FATED TO THE BEAST

KENZIE SKYE

CHAPTER
ONE

Fiona

I pull my cloak closer about me and shudder with more than winter's chill when I think of Lord Fairchild. I know my father means well and he only wants to make sure I'm taken care of when he's gone, but I do desperately wish he would stop trying to set me up with all these rich old toads.

I'm not a vain woman, and of course I know the ways of the world for women of my ilk. I know the best hope for women of my social standing is to marry a well-to-do man. And it's not like I'm asking for the most handsome man in the world, but I'm filled with repulsion every time I think of a man who's older than my father putting his wrinkled hands all over me.

I know that's the way it is around here, though. Most of the young brides are married off to men old enough to be their fathers because they're the ones with all the money to afford a young, beautiful bride.

I don't want to marry at all. If I have my way, I'll spend the rest of my days alone in a little cottage here in the forest. I'm smart enough to take care of myself. My father taught me basic survival skills, and Greta taught me all I need to know about what herbs and foods are safe for consumption. I know how to set a trap too, so I could catch me a hare every now and then and some other little critters to eat.

I don't need or want to be chained to a husband. Convincing my father of that is another story, though. He already worries about me not having a mother figure to guide me.

My fingers move up to my neck in a habitual movement to grasp the amulet she gave me before she died of sickness when I was only eight years old.

I frown when my fingertips brush bare flesh

and I realize I forgot to wear my necklace today. I never forget to put on my amulet, but I was so distressed when I heard Lord Fairchild's voice floating through the walls that I was in haste to make a quick escape.

When I emerged from my room to find the overbearing gentleman sitting at the table with my father, I came up with the excuse that I had to go gather berries.

It's not exactly a lie. I've gathered at least enough berries for a blueberry pie. But the main reason I came up with that excuse is because I knew there was no way Lord Fairchild would offer to accompany me.

A stout gentleman with a potbelly, he's not keen on exercise. The one time he insisted on accompanying me on one of my excursions through the forest, big, disgusting beads of sweat rolled down his face when we were only five minutes into the walk. His pudgy chest had huffed and puffed with exertion, and he'd bid us go back before he became more winded.

No, Lord Fairchild prefers to sit indoors, preferably over a mug of ale and a bowl of meat stew.

It's not just that Lord Fairchild is old and gray

and fat either. We have absolutely nothing in common. He prefers to be indoors, whereas I prefer to be outdoors. He likes to sit idle, whereas I like to keep busy.

Oh, there have been plenty of younger candidates who've come sniffing around too, wanting to put in their offers for my hand in marriage. Some of them are quite handsome. But still, no one has caught my fancy in that way and made me eager to lose my status as a maiden.

My fingers trail over my bare throat as I mindlessly reach for my amulet again.

The stone has never glowed either.

I'm starting to seriously doubt if it ever will.

At this point, it's fine by me if it doesn't.

Being married isn't about what I want anyway. I know that. It's about my father securing my future.

I scowl as I bend down and savagely pluck some more berries from a vine I find stretching across the ground.

I hate the inevitability of being married off to the highest bidder.

I instantly chastise myself for my unkind thoughts. I know that's not fair. My father isn't trying to make the most money he can off me. He truly does have my best interests at heart. I just wish he would listen to me when I tell him I have no desire to marry. Instead, he just nods at me in that fatherly, condescending way of his like he's humoring a petulant child who doesn't know what's best for her.

"You're young yet, Fiona," he always says, "but trust me when I say you'll thank me when you have a warm hearth and plenty of food in your belly when you're married to a man of substance. A man who can give you more than your old dad ever could."

"You're just as beautiful as your mother was." Tears always shimmer in his eyes when he talks about her. Father has never wed again. He loved my mother so.

My heart aches at the memory of her. If I ever do get married, I want to marry for love like she and he did, but my father will hear nothing of that.

"You're so beautiful, Fiona. You've got options. You don't want to make the same mistake your poor mother, God bless her soul, did. She married me, a pauper, for love. And look where that got her."

He always looks so heartbroken when he

admits that, and it hurts me when my father talks like that. I know he still blames himself for my mother's death.

When she came down with the sickness, we didn't have the money for doctors to treat her. My father has convinced himself that if he hadn't been so selfish when they were courting, if he'd let her go, that she would have married a richer man and she'd still be here today.

Maybe that's true, but would she have been happy? At least while she was here, she was completely in love.

I sigh again, and the sound seems to echo all around me.

I suddenly notice that all the chirping of the birds has died away, and there's an ominous chill in the air. I look up and see that I've wandered farther into the forest than I usually do. I was so lost in my thoughts I wasn't really paying attention to where I was going.

I look to the left and the right, my brow furrowing as I try to remember which way I came from.

Everything seems forebodingly quiet here—like there's a hush in the air. The trees are so dense and thick that they block out all the sunlight, casting the mossy forest floor in gloom and shadow.

Prickles of awareness cause the hairs on the back of my neck to stand up. A shiver runs down my spine as I suddenly sense that I'm not alone.

I hear a low growl rumble behind me, and I turn around slowly, my heart thumping steadily in my chest.

My eyes widen as my head tilts up.

I gasp and take a step back, the basket slipping from my grasp.

Berries spill across the ground, and I feel them squelching underneath my boots as I squash them in my hasty retreat.

Their purple juices leak out to stain the hem of my dress, but I pay it no mind.

My eyes are locked on the creature looming over me, and fear holds me in its sharp grasp as I realize I'm in deep trouble.

It's the Beast of Boding.

CHAPTER
TWO

Broderick

The tiny little female in front of me drops the basket of berries she was stealing from my land and gasps as she looks up at me.

My snarl fades away as I'm hit with the most beautiful sapphire blue eyes I've ever seen. She takes a step back from me, her eyes widening in fear, and my anger flares again.

Anger at my entire situation. Half man, half beast, I've never fit in anywhere. That's why I stick to myself. Seeing this beautiful human's fear of me reminds me of that stark fact.

I know what she sees when she looks up at me. A beast that has the semblance of a man yet also that of a mix between a bear and a wolf.

I force myself to calm down, knowing that if I do, I'll go back to my wholly human appearance.

It's only when I become angry that my animal side comes out, showing me for the hidden beast I truly am.

"The Beast of Boding," she whispers to herself in amazement. She's still staring up at me agape. Her brow furrows as I calm and morph back down into my human form.

I grimace at the moniker. I've never cared that the townsfolk called me the Beast of Boding. In fact, it serves my purposes well because it means they stay far away from me and don't give me any trouble, but for some reason, hearing the title coming from this beautiful little human's lips bothers me. I don't like the thought that she sees me as a beast—even if that is what I really am.

I'm still towering over her. I'm abnormally large for a human, but at least I look more normal in this form anyway.

She cocks her little head to the side and looks up at me inquisitively, all her earlier fear seemingly forgotten in the face of her curiosity. "But how..." she begins before she clears her throat and goes on, "How are you human too?"

Her assumption that I stay in my beastly form all the time, as if I'm less than human, angers me all over again.

But I make an effort to breathe in deeply to keep myself from morphing back into my beastly state.

As I inhale deep breaths, I scent her. My entire body goes rigid as her unique smell teases my nostrils. She smells utterly feminine, like roses and lilies. A heady and intoxicating mix of innocence and purity and sensuality.

My eyes roll over her from head to toe. She's such a tiny little thing with long, dark hair that flows down to her waist. Her little lips are plush and pink, and those beautiful sapphire eyes are framed by dark, thick lashes. A porcelain complexion gives her a cherubic look.

She's far too pretty to be out here in these woods unescorted.

I feel my cock hardening, my body reacting to both her scent and her visceral beauty.

I've been alone for too many years. I've long since given up on finding a mate, but it's obvious that my body recognizes the scent of a woman.

I'm suddenly pulsing with desire. I want this woman with every fiber of my being. Every instinct within me is telling me to claim her here and now.

Thoughts tumble through my head as I weigh my options.

I could keep her. Take her for my mate. She's pretty and I want her. I'm tired of being alone.

But what if she refuses me? I look down at her lustfully. Of course, she'll refuse me. I'm half beast, and she's fucking beautiful.

I could take her by force. I'm ashamed that I even consider it. It just goes to show how depraved I really am that the thought even flits through my mind. If I mate her by force, I truly would be turning over to the inner beast inside me.

While I struggle with my internal debate, she begins inching away from me, her eyes looking up at me warily, no doubt put on guard by the potent lust written all over my face.

I become anxious at the thought of her leaving and never seeing her again. Desperation wells up within me, so I lash out at her, "You were stealing from me."

Her eyes widen, and she shakes her head in

immediate denial. "No, I was just out gathering berries."

"You trespassed on my land," I growl at her. If I were to treat her just like anyone else, there would be dire consequences for her offenses.

"I didn't realize how far I'd gotten," she protests. "I was deep in thought."

"About what?" I growl, internally cursing myself for wanting so desperately to know what she was thinking of that caused her to stray so far. Does she even realize she entered territory that no other humans dare venture into?

"Marriage," she answers softly.

"Marriage?" I grind out, my chest tightening and my vision going red at the thought of another man claiming her.

I feel my body struggling to shift again, but I calm myself, not wanting to scare her any more than I already have.

"Are you betrothed?" I demand to know. I suddenly *need* to know.

She takes another cautious step back from me as she shakes her head. "Not yet, and I don't want to be either."

"What's your name?" she suddenly asks me.

I blink in surprise. How long has it been since someone has asked me that?

I let out a mirthless chuckle when I remember her whispering the townspeople's moniker for me. "Haven't you heard? I'm the Beast of Boding." My voice is like flint, and many a man has trembled to hear that tone in my voice.

But not this little creature.

She shakes her head, her eyes looking up at me with softness. My chest squeezes painfully as an unfamiliar feeling of discomfort washes over me. "That can't be your real name," she says softly.

I look down at her, and my heart—that organ that I thought long since dead—starts beating in my chest. This tiny little human isn't afraid of me. And she's asking what my name is.

"Broderick," I finally answer her gruffly.

"Broderick," she repeats my name, and the sound of it coming from her sweet lips does some-thing to me. A ball forms deep in my belly, and I want nothing more than to pick her up and feel her in my arms.

"I'm Fiona," she tells me. I stare down at her in amazement, unbelieving that she offered her name to me so freely.

"Fiona," I taste her name on my lips for the first time. Nothing has ever tasted so right.

She smiles up at me then, the sweet, innocent creature, and it's like a sucker punch straight to my gut. I can't breathe for a second as I take in her beauty. It's like the sun has finally come out and shone light down on my dark day.

And that's what cements my decision. Without another word, I stalk over to her, watching her face as her eyes go wide again as I approach her.

I bend down and throw her over my shoulder.

"What are you doing?" she gasps.

"I'm taking you home with me," I tell her frankly.

She starts to protest, her little legs and fists kicking. Although her feet don't connect with anything, her fists hammer me on the back, but it's just as irritating as a fly buzzing around my head. It does me no damage at all.

"Wait, Broderick!" I love the sound of my name dripping from her lips, and a smile plays on my lips at the thought of hearing it more. She might be angry with me at first, but surely, she'll get over it in time, and even if she doesn't, having her anger will be better than nothing. I can't bear the thought of releasing her now. Not when every-thing inside me is screaming that she's mine.

"Put me down! You can't just take me like this!" She's still kicking and screaming.

I ignore her and stalk all the way back to my gates. I can, and I will because for once in my life, I've found something good—something that I want to keep—and I'm taking it.

This little human—*Fiona*—is now mine.

THREE

Fiona

"Broderick!" I scream the beast's name as I aim a kick at his head. He dodges it easily and just grunts and hoists me up higher on his shoulder like I'm a sack of potatoes.

I finally give up and stop fighting when I realize that it's not going to do any good. There's no way I can get away from this huge mountain of a man. Although not quite as big as he was in his beastly form, he's still much larger than the average man.

It was stupid of me to underestimate him, but I

thought I saw a sliver of humanity in him when I asked him his name. He looked so shocked that I asked him, and that caused my heart to twist within me in pity.

How long has it been since someone was decent enough to him to ask him his name? The thought of him all alone and denied the basest of human kindness causes my naturally compassionate nature to rise up within me. I'd wanted nothing more than to be kind to him.

Yes, my initial reaction to him was fear, but now, even though he's got me flung over his shoulder and is obviously kidnapping me, somehow deep inside me, I don't feel like he'll truly hurt me.

I don't know why I feel that way, but I do. Maybe I'm just a stupid girl who can't sense danger when it's right in front of her. That's surely what my papa would say if he could see me now.

My heart twists at the thought of my papa. He's going to be so worried when I don't come home. There's no telling what he's going to think happened to me. He'll likely think I was killed in the woods.

Anxiety beats in my breast at my next thought.

What if he thinks I'm upset with him and I ran away? He knows I don't want to be married.

The thought is like a knife twisting deep inside me when I imagine him feeling guilty like that. He already feels guilty enough about Mama's death. I don't want him to feel guilty about my disappearance too.

I have to get home to him and ease his fears. I'm all he has.

"Look, Broderick," I try another tactic, speaking in a calm, even voice even though I'm still flung over his shoulder ungracefully. "People are going to come looking for me when I don't go back."

He merely grunts by way of acknowledgment, and it's obvious by that grunt that he's completely unconcerned.

"My papa will worry about me," I try again. "They'll probably send out a search party," I warn him, "and then all those people will be trespassing on your property."

Surely that will be enough to upset him. He got so angry when he found just little ole' me trespassing on his property. Imagine how he'd be if there were tons of people on his land uninvited.

And surely there will be some sort of search party.

While I'm not necessarily the most popular girl in the village, I am very well-liked, and there are several men who would love to find me if only for the chance to be my champion and get a head-up on having my hand in marriage. I grimace. I can definitely see my papa offering my hand to the man who rescues me.

On second thought, maybe I'll be better off to take my chances with Broderick.

Then, it suddenly occurs to me that I don't know what Broderick wants with me. He just flung me over his shoulder and started taking off with me, and I haven't even asked where he's taking me or what he plans on doing to me. What's wrong with me that I don't feel more imminent danger than I do?

"Broderick, put me down, please," I ask him as evenly as I can, using his name to try to appeal to his humanity."

"No," his big chest rumbles with the word. "You'll run if I do."

I should be angry that he's capturing me, but instead, I'm still feeling pity at the thought that he's so afraid I'll run from him. I don't imagine anyone has ever voluntarily stayed near him before.

"I won't," I insist. "I promise. It's just all the blood is rushing to my head with me slung over your shoulder this way, and I'm starting to feel a little dizzy." It's not a complete lie. It's definitely uncomfortable being flung over his big shoulder like this.

That seems to do the trick because the next thing I know Broderick slides me around to his front and cradles me in his arms in compromise.

Okay, so he didn't set me down on my feet, but this is better, I suppose.

I look up at him, and I'm startled by the full impact of his eyes up close. They're a beautiful silvery gray like the bark on the trees or the storm clouds rolling in.

His brows pull down as he looks at me in concern. I feel my breath catching in my throat. They might call him the Beast of Boding, but this man isn't as beastly as many I've met trying to secure my hand in marriage.

Yeah, he might be technically kidnapping me right now, but I don't feel in danger of my life, and he seems to be showing concern for me if the way he cradles my head in his hand that's more like a big paw is any indication.

"Is that better?" His chest rumbles, and I feel the vibration run clean through me.

"Yes," I admit, but I can't help adding, "but I really can walk, and I won't run off."

He just grunts again by way of answer and tightens his arms around me possessively— almost as if he doesn't like the thought of putting me down.

"Where are you taking me?" I finally ask him

"I told you," he answers without looking down at me. "Home."

My heart begins to beat harder in my chest. "Why?"

He doesn't answer, and he keeps his jaw squared as he looks straight ahead and continues to march toward his destination.

It suddenly strikes me that maybe he's lonely. All the townspeople fear him, so there's no telling how long he's lived out here all alone.

My heart tugs within me at the thought. If all he wants is some company, maybe my little bit of kindness was enough to make him want to keep me.

I bite my lip as I consider my dilemma. While he might be a bit terrifying in his beastly form that looks like a mixture between a bear and a wolf, he's ruggedly handsome in his human form, with untamed brown hair that falls down to his shoulders and his gray eyes that hold more humanity in them than most men I've met.

From the tales I grew up hearing of him, he's a monster. Everyone makes him out to be a rabid beast, but I can't help thinking of animals that turn feral when they're backed into a corner and equating Broderick to that. If all anyone has ever seen is his beastly side, maybe it's because that's all he's ever been incentivized to show them.

"Broderick," I try again, appealing to the gentle side I've seen in him, "You have to let me go. I need to go home to my papa. I promise I won't say anything about you. No one will ever bother you."

A muscle in his jaw ticks, and his nostrils flare. I see the storm clouds rolling in his eyes as his face seems to begin to morph from man to beast. I stiffen in his arms, suddenly afraid of him once more.

He closes his eyes and takes in a deep breath, and the transition fades away. I blink, looking up at him incredulously like maybe I imagined it, yet I know I didn't.

His temper is that volatile. A shiver runs through me at the thought that he could turn in just an instant like that. Maybe I should fear him after all.

"No," he barks, and I flinch at his tone. We finally reach an old iron gate covered with ivy. It squeaks eerily when Broderick opens it. He closes it behind us and latches it with finality. I feel my heart sink.

I glance up at the ominous-looking castle in front of us. Its stone exterior is foreboding and gray and dark and lifeless. If this is where he lives, no wonder his mood is so dour. The place looks like it would suck the mirth right out of the jolliest soul.

"You will not leave here, Fiona." His voice is cold and stern and brooks no argument. It causes my stomach to drop within me. I look up at him and see nothing but hardness in his eyes. All semblance of the gentle giant I thought I glimpsed before is gone, and a shiver of the fear I should have felt all along runs down my spine.

It seems like maybe I was wrong about him after all.

Broderick truly is a beast, and he's just effectively captured me.

FOUR

Broderick

Fiona shrinks into me and huddles closer to my chest, though I'm sure she's not even aware she's doing it. It's just a reaction to her fear of my decrepit-looking castle.

I glance up at the weathered gray stones. It is pretty ominous looking with its dark pallor and all the vines climbing up its facade. I have to admit that, but it's functional and has always provided a safe home for me, and it'll be a safe home for her too. She'll see that in time.

Plus, what she doesn't realize is that the foreboding exterior isn't indicative of the interior. I like to think the interior of my home is warm and inviting, and I keep beautiful gardens out back filled with roses, lilies, lavender, chrysanthemum, and various other flora. I seem to have a green thumb, and I'll take beauty wherever I can get it since I am anything but beautiful. While I have a gardener, I often like to the tend to the plants myself. A little hobby, if you will.

As far as my home goes, maybe I like the subconscious symbolism of the ugly exterior having a beautiful interior—not like that analogy applies to me. I'm a beast through and through, and I've accepted that for the most part. The hard exterior of my castle serves another purpose as well. It keeps unwanted guests away too.

Regardless of the reason, I love the feeling of Fiona pressing closer to me, and my arms tighten about her instinctively in response.

I make a conscious effort to relax them, not wanting to harm her by squeezing her too tightly. I'm not used to holding another human and am often unaware of my strength. And she's such a tiny, delicate little thing. Her slender throat catches my gaze. It would be too easy to snap it in two. I must handle her with care.

When we reach the door, it swings open, and I see my butler's eyes widen as he takes in the woman in my arms.

"Have Belinda prepare a room for our guest," I order him tersely. I can see the questions in his eyes, but the look on my face keeps him from uttering them.

"Of course, my lord. Right away," he says as he holds the door open for us to pass through.

Once we're securely in my castle with the doors closed behind us, I finally, reluctantly, set Fiona down on her feet.

She runs her hands down over her blue dress, absently smoothing the folds. "You have servants?" she asks me, the surprise in her voice obvious.

And that irritates me just like it irritated me when she thought I stayed in my beastly form all the time.

"As hard as it is to believe, some people will tolerate my company," I growl at her.

She blinks, taken aback by my tone, before uttering softly, "That's not what I meant at all."

I inwardly curse myself for snapping at her. I gentle my voice as I hold out a hand to her. "Would you like me to show you around?"

She looks up at me and hesitates before she finally places her hand in mine.

I take it as a victory when she touches me of her own free will. Well, she might feel like she has to, but she placed her hand in mine voluntarily. I didn't forcibly take it. And that has to count for something.

I have to fight the urge to sweep her back up in my arms and cradle her to my chest again. I want to carry her everywhere just to feel her close to me, but I realize that's not normal human behavior. So, I refrain—no matter how difficult it is.

She's quiet as I give her a tour of the place, and I feel my anxiety rising within me again. Why did I ever think this would work? She's never going to warm up to me. I've kidnapped her and forced her here.

I am more beast than human. Everyone's right to call me the beast that I am. Filled with self-loathing, my countenance quickly sours.

"You're free to roam the castle, but you're not to leave these walls without my permission. If you want to see the grounds, ask me and I'll take you," I lay down the ground rules impassively.

What's done is done, and I'm keeping her.

She peers up at me with a frown before she

tentatively pleads yet again, "Broderick, please don't do this. You can't keep me here."

Hearing her sweet voice saying my name while begging for her freedom once again causes something within me to snap. Is she that eager to get away from me? Is my presence that loathsome to her?

I should have known she's just like everyone else. The small acts of kindness she showed me back in the forest were probably nothing more than her attempt at charming the beast long enough so she could get away.

I'm such a fucking fool for thinking otherwise.

Still, that doesn't abate the desire coursing hotly through my veins, and the mix of anger and lust makes for a violently potent cocktail.

"You will never leave here, Fiona!" I snarl at her. "The sooner you accept that fact, the easier your life will be!"

She finally bursts out herself," What do you want with me?"

Those sapphire blue eyes of hers are blazing with her own anger, and her face is flushed.

My god, she looks beautiful when she's in a temper.

I suddenly grab her and pull her little body

flush against mine. Her eyes widen as she feels my throbbing erection between us, leaving no doubt in her mind as to exactly what I want with her. She knows now.

She trembles against me, and I release her abruptly, cursing and disgusted with myself. I run my hands through my hair.

Here she is an innocent young maiden—a virgin—and I'm thrusting my big cock against her. No wonder she's scared witless.

Despite her fear, I can still feel the press of her body against mine, and I want desperately to pull her back to me and hump her little mound. I ball my hands into fists and clench my teeth together so tightly I'm surprised I don't shatter my jaw. My eyes are probably wild with the desperate hunger I feel for her.

I take in a deep breath to calm myself, but that only revs me up even more whenever I'm assaulted by her sweet scent—the scent of a perfect little virgin, and she's right here within my grasp.

I have to get away from her now before I ravish her right here on the bearskin rug of my library. Before I lose all control and do something that I'll surely regret, I turn swiftly on my heels and stalk from the room.

Why did I ever bring her here? I'm torturing myself, but the thought of setting her free causes a knife to twist deep in my gut.

I let out a roar as I finally allow myself to shift into my beastly form and hit the grounds for a hard run. I need to work off some of this adrenaline.

Fiona

I flinch when I hear Broderick's deafening roar sounding from down the hallway. It sounds so loud even while it sounds far away.

My face is still flushed from feeling his arousal pressing against my body. If I had any doubts about what Broderick wanted from me, I don't anymore.

I don't know much about men, but I'm fairly certain that Broderick is more than well-endowed. What he pressed against me felt huge. I know the mechanics of how the sexual acts works, and I can't imagine how anything that large could fit inside me. He'd split me in two!

And while that thought should completely horrify me—and does a bit—I feel a throbbing between my legs even now. I also feel wetness pooling between my thighs, and that only makes me flush deeper.

What does that mean? Does that mean my body recognizes his call and wants him too? I remember the feeling of being held in his arms, and I can't deny that it wasn't a totally unpleasant experience. No, it actually felt really good being cradled against Broderick's massive chest.

He held me so gently—like I was made of glass and he was afraid of breaking me.

Broderick might look and act like a beast, but he's got a tender side too. Still, that doesn't mean that he's not also dangerous when provoked. I'm starkly reminded of that fact when I hear another frightening roar sounding throughout the castle.

I jump, but not from Broderick's roar. A feminine voice startles me.

"Are you ready for me to show you to your room, Miss?" The voice is kindly and crackles with age.

I turn around to see a woman with her hair

pulled back into a gray bun staring down at me. She's taller than me, though it doesn't take much to be taller than me, and wearing a maid's uniform complete with a starched white apron. Her soft brown eyes are lined with wrinkles, but her face is pleasant and welcoming. Her easy countenance puts me at ease immediately.

"Sure," I tell her. "My name's Fiona."

She smiles at me, her eyes lighting up. "I'm Belinda, the head of housekeeping here. We haven't had any guests since the late Master Boding passed." Her eyes take on a saddened look. "I'm afraid the young master isn't much for company." Then her eyes light up again when she turns and surveys me anew. "But I'm so happy to see that he's finally having a guest."

I hesitate to tell her that I'm not a guest, that I'm, in fact, a prisoner. For some reason, I'm hesitant to stomp all over her happy view of her master. Even if she did know I was a prisoner, what would it accomplish? No servant will turn against their master and risk losing their job to help a stranger.

So, I ultimately decide to keep my true state of being here to myself. There's no need to bring this kind woman down. I'll find a way out of the mess, and I won't risk involving any of Broderick's loyal staff.

I just smile at her, opting for silence. That way I'm not technically lying to the woman either.

She must take my smile as confirmation of her assumption because she turns and beckons me to follow her. "This way, dear."

Belinda chatters on as she leads me down several corridors. I try to remember every twist and turn we take, but I fear I'll never remember the way out of this castle.

I can't help wondering if Broderick purposefully worked it out where I'd be put in rooms so deep within the castle that I'd get lost trying to find my way out.

Another roar sounds. This time it sounds like it's outside the castle.

Belinda casts a nervous glance over her shoulder at me before she assures me, "The master can get into a temper sometimes, but I promise you, he's really a very gentle soul.

I've already gathered as much, but I'm still not totally convinced that Broderick can't be dangerous too, so again I say nothing.

"Well, here you are, dear." Belinda flings open

a door, and my eyes widen in surprise as I take in the opulence of the room.

It's grander than anything I've ever seen, with damask curtains and bedding. A fire roars cheerily in the big stone fireplace, the wood crackling.

Belinda hovers in the doorway before she finally speaks again. "Is everything to your liking, Miss?"

"Oh yes," I rush to assure her. "Of course! It's amazing. Thank you, Belinda." I smile at her kindly, and she nods her head, a smile of satisfaction on her face before she tells me with a guarded tone, "Chef has prepared a meal, but perhaps it's best if you take it here in your room since the master is out. Unless you prefer to eat in the dining room alone?" She raises her eyebrow inquisitively, though it's obvious she thinks I'd prefer to be alone up here rather than alone in the dining hall.

Though I actually would, I decide against cowering here in this room. Besides, if I have her escort me down to the dining hall, that gives me another chance to get my bearings about me and memorize my way out of this castle.

I raise my chin as I tell her, "Actually, I'd love to eat in the dining hall since your chef has already gone to all the trouble to prepare a meal for me. If it's not too much trouble, of course."

Belinda blinks and looks taken aback before a genuine smile lights up her face. "Wonderful, Miss. Chef will be delighted to hear it. Why don't you freshen up a bit while I go tell him to make the preparations, and then I'll be back to collect you?"

I nod my assent and then make my way over to the water basin once the door clicks shut behind her.

I dip my hands into the warm water and then proceed to wet my face and neck. I can't deny the comforts in Broderick's castle. It's much warmer and more inviting on the inside than it is on the outside.

My thoughts shift back to the master himself, and curiosity teases at me. Who is he? He's the Beast of Boding. I know that, but who is he *really*? How did he become whatever he is? Some sort of shifter? I've heard the townspeople talk about those who could shift from a human to animal form, but I admit that I chalked it all up to fairy-tales, having never seen such a person myself.

I wonder who Broderick's parents were and if they had the same half human-half animal state Broderick does.

I remember how terrifying Broderick looked in his beastly state, yet I'm curious to see him in that state again to get a closer look at him.

I shake my head. Something's obviously wrong with me. I should be plotting my escape, yet instead, I'm pondering over my captor and how I'd like to study his beastly form more.

My silent reverie is broken when Belinda returns true to her word to collect me and lead me down to the dining hall.

This time I make sure to pay close attention to each turn, and while I think I can remember my way to the dining hall now, I'm still no closer to knowing where the front door is. I don't know where the dining hall is in position to the front door or whether I'm still deep into the castle or any closer to the front door or not.

The dining table is huge. It looks long enough to seat at least a hundred people—if not more, and I can't help thinking what a waste it must be to have such accommodations and yet never have any guests to use them with.

A thought of Broderick sitting at the head of this table and eating all alone tugs at my heart.

I scowl at myself. I need to stop feeling sorry for my captor. I don't have to hate him, but I also need to remember that he's holding me here against my will, and no amount of pity will negate that fact or make his actions okay.

Since the master of the house is missing in action, I'm seated at the head of the table where the chef dotes on me, watching my face with pleasure for any reaction. I make sure to praise his efforts, and it's really not difficult because the food is delicious—much better than any fare I've ever eaten before.

By the way the chef is hanging on to my every praise, I'm guessing he doesn't get much chance to put his skills to good use here, nor is he used to praise. In fact, the entire staff around here is so attentive, they all remind me of neglected animals jumping at the first show of attention.

Just as I'm telling Chef I can't eat another bite, the door slams open, and a soaking wet Broderick is standing there.

He's dripping from head to toe, so either it started raining or he's jumped into a body of water somewhere.

The wet strands of his brown hair are hanging down his shoulders, and his wet shirt and pants are molded against his rock-hard body. I can see his strong, chiseled pectorals and abs through the way his shirt is clinging to his body, and I try not to stare.

He looks magnificent. Raw, powerful, beautiful. Like a dangerous creature to be admired from afar.

His gray eyes almost seem to glow silver, though he's back in his human form, and those eyes are honed right in on me sitting in his chair.

I flush and make as if to rise, but before I can, he turns on his heel and stomps out of the dining room.

My back stiffens when I hear a door slam. He's obviously still "in his temper," as Belinda had so aptly put it.

Well, to hell with him. I didn't ask to be here, and he can't expect me and his staff to just know what he wants or when he'll return from raging in the woods.

I don't really care if he's upset by finding me sitting at the head of his table like I own the damn place.

In fact, I hope he is.

Maybe if I piss him off enough, he'll let me go.

It's a far cry, but I suddenly decide that I'm not going to be the docile prisoner and make things easy on him.

Fiona

I try to get a bit of sleep to prepare me for my journey, but of course, I toss and turn without catching one wink.

I'm just too nervous and wound up. I don't really think Broderick will hurt me if he catches me trying to escape, but I also don't want to find out either. I just want to get the hell out of here and back home to my father.

When it's been completely silent in the castle for a couple of hours and I no longer hear the pitter-patter of any of the staff's footsteps falling outside my chamber door, I slip out of the bed. I'm still completely dressed in anticipation of my impending escape.

I keep my footfalls quiet as I creep over to the doorway. I open it slowly, peeking my head out to look up and down the corridor.

The only thing I see is the flickering of the flames in the candelabras that line both sides of the hallway.

So, I tentatively step out of the door, taking care to close it behind me slowly to keep it from creaking.

I let out a breath I didn't realize I was holding when I'm finally all the way out of the room and into the hallway.

I begin creeping slowly down the corridor, stopping every few steps to make sure I don't hear any noises.

I know my goal is to get out of here unseen, but my curiosity starts to get the best of me as I make my way through the castle. I find myself stopping to admire the tapestries on the wall. I peek into several rooms to see them all decorated in different hues. I wonder what the castle was like once upon a time when it was teeming with guests.

I finally come upon an opulent-looking door with beautiful engraving on the molding. All the woodwork looks so intricate, and I can't help wondering what must be behind such a grand entryway.

I push the door softly open and then freeze when I see Broderick's completely naked body standing in the moonlight.

Every muscle in his huge form is bulging and clearly defined. His legs are like cannons, his buttocks round and hard, and I see the muscles rippling in his arms as his hand moves up and down.

His back is turned to me, so I watch in amazement as the muscles on his back flex too.

He's breathtakingly gorgeous with the moonlight highlighting him like this.

He turns a fraction of an inch, and I gasp when I see what he's doing.

Oh my.

He's stroking the huge column of flesh that's jutting out from between his thighs. It's impossibly thick and long and so swollen that I can see the veins popping out of it. The head is purple and leaking a clear, milky looking substance.

I've never seen a man's member before, and I

can't tear my eyes away from Broderick's throbbing flesh.

His hand is moving up and down it so quickly it's almost a blur, and then his whole body tenses as he throws his head back and groans. That groan is a deep, guttural sound that comes straight from his belly, and for some reason, it makes my heart skip a beat.

I clench my thighs together in an unconscious effort to ease the sudden throbbing there as I watch Broderick's erect member jerk in his hand, releasing thick ropes of white liquid into the air.

My body is flushed as I realize what I just witnessed, and I turn on my heel and run before he discovers my voyeurism.

I don't know which direction I'm running. I've lost all sense of direction. I no longer pause to admire any of the beautiful architecture or peek into rooms. My only instinct is to flee as quickly as I can. I can't even say why seeing Broderick self-pleasuring himself triggered my panic button—only that the sight made my body feel amazing and terrifying things, and my instinctual reaction is to run from them.

I don't know how long I run. Time seems to

lose all meaning, but finally, I see it. The front door.

I redouble my efforts and make a beeline for it. I'm so close to freedom I can taste it.

My heart rate picks up and hope lights in my chest.

But it's like someone has dropped a stone right into my belly when a big hand slams onto the door in front of me.

I suddenly feel a warm presence behind me, and I don't even have to turn around to know who that big hand belongs to. An earthy, masculine scent invades my nostrils, and my body begins to quake.

"Going somewhere, little bird?" Broderick's voice is a warning and a caress all at once, and I can't stop the shiver that goes down my spine when I feel his hot breath on the side of my neck. I hear him inhale, and somehow, I know even without seeing him that he's turned his head in toward me to smell my hair.

I start to move to the left, but his other hand slaps onto the door. With his arms on either side of me, I'm effectively caged in between his massive chest and the equally massive door.

"Broderick, please," I stammer, though I'm not even sure what I'm asking for at this point.

I never get a chance to finish my plea because just like he did in the woods, Broderick suddenly lifts me and slings me over his shoulder.

Panic flares in my chest again. "I'm sorry, Broderick. I wasn't really going to leave. I swear it!"

A chuckle rumbles through his big body, but he sounds anything but amused. "Little liar," he comments as he stalks back up the stairs with me.

I assume he's going to take me back to my room and lock me up in there this time, so I'm perplexed when he finally sets me down in a room that's not the one I was staying in.

I look around in confusion when I realize that he placed me in the room where I caught him pleasuring himself.

My cheeks flush at the memory, and by the way his gray eyes are glowing almost silver down at me, I have a feeling that maybe he knows I caught him.

I stand there like an animal backed into a corner, especially when he closes the big heavy door behind him. It shuts with an ominous thud as he turns back to look down at me.

I swallow before asking, "What are you going to do with me?"

His lips thin, and his nostrils flare as his eyes rake over my form.

"Nothing," he finally says before he walks over to the huge bed and begins unbuttoning his shirt.

I just stare at him warily, thankful and disappointed all at once when he keeps his breeches on.

He glances over at me and raises an eyebrow. "Well?"

"Well, what?" I ask him cautiously.

"Are you coming to bed or not?"

My eyes widen, and he scowls at me. "Not for that. To sleep, little bird."

I don't know when his nickname for me was born, but something about it calms me. If he thinks enough of me to come up with a nickname for me, then surely, he has no plans to kill me.

"You mean...sleep with you?" I twist my hands together nervously. I've never slept with a man before, much less one as big and intimidating as Broderick.

"I obviously can't trust you in your own room, and forgive me if I don't feel like standing guard outside your door all night to make sure you don't run away." His voice is low and growly.

My face flushes at his berating tone, and I have to fight the urge to tell him I'm sorry because why should I be sorry? He's the one who's kidnapped me and is keeping me here against my will. I, on the other hand, haven't done anything wrong.

He sighs when I make no move to come any closer to him or the bed. He comes over to me and then turns me before I feel him undoing the buttons at the back of my dress.

I jerk away from him and turn back around. "What are you doing?"

He sighs again before he answers patiently, "Helping you get out of this dress. Surely you don't want to sleep fully dressed. Don't women only sleep in their shifts?"

I nod but then shake my head at him. "Yes, they do, but, no, I don't want to get undressed. I'm fine like I am."

He frowns down at me, and then his eyes heat as he leans closer to tell me. "If I wanted to ravish you, Fiona, no amount of clothing would stop me."

My breath hitches in my throat as I stare up into his stormy gray eyes.

"I give you my word that I won't take you against your will," his rumbling voice vows.

I search his eyes and relax when I see the truth

in them. Broderick means what he says, and I believe him. He won't force himself on me.

The only problem is what if my traitorous body wants him to? My face flushes at the thought, and Broderick smirks down at me as if he can read my thoughts.

I turn my back to him, partly to hide my flaming cheeks from him and to let him continue unbuttoning my dress.

I can't believe I'm going to sleep next to the Beast of Boding.

SEVEN

Broderick

My blood is thrumming through my veins as I undo the delicate little buttons on the back of Fiona's dress. I know she could manage them on her own, but when she turned and presented her back to me, I wasn't about to turn down the opportunity to touch her—no matter how minuscule.

My fingers brush against her soft skin, and my mouth goes dry at the expanse of creamy white neck that's revealed to me when she pulls her hair over one shoulder to allow me better access to her.

Her shift is so thin I can almost see her skin clean through it. She's obviously aware of this fact if the way she keeps her back turned to me is any indication.

It doesn't matter if I can see her or not. Just the thought of her rosy little nipples and pink little mound is enough to have me rock hard again. Everything about her keeps me in a state of constant desire. Her scent, the delicate way she moves.

I want to taste her more than I want my next breath. It takes every ounce of self-control I have not to turn her in my arms and pull her flush against me.

She keeps her back to me as she edges awkwardly to the bed with her hands crossed up to her neck to protect her nipples from my gaze.

Only when she slides under the covers and pulls them up to her chin do I get in on the other side.

I can't help but chuckle when I see she's on the edge of the bed as far away from me as she can get. *Oh, little bird, you have no idea.*

I reach across the bed and pull her unceremoniously to me until we're spooning with her back against my front.

Fuck, she's so warm and soft that I instantly feel the flesh between my legs begin to swell with desire.

"What are you doing, Broderick?" Her voice is shaky and breathy, and I feel her trembling against me.

"You don't think I trust you not to slip out of bed once I fall asleep, do you? This way I know you won't be slipping off in the middle of the night," I whisper against her ear as I band my arm around her, knowing there's no way she'll ever be able to budge me when I'm completely wrapped around her like this.

Plus, I'd be lying if I said I'm not looking for any excuse to hold her. I'm actually glad she tried to run because this gives me a reason to keep her close to me. She's now officially a flight risk, and there's no way I'm letting my little bird get away from me.

"But..." she begins trying to wiggle out of my hold, and that puts her sweet little arse grinding right against my erection.

I can't stop the groan that leaves my lips. "Keep that up, and you're going to make me rethink my promise to you, Fiona," I warn her.

She goes completely still, and I halfway want to weep at the loss of the sensation.

"Broderick..." she begins again, but I shush her.

"Silence, Fiona," my voice cracks with all the sexual tension I feel. "It's either this or the dungeon. Your pick." I'm pretty sure I know what her answer will be, but I hold my breath while I wait for her acquiescence.

I release it when she stays silent. I don't know what I'd have done if she'd actually sassed back that she'd prefer the dungeon because I can't stomach the thought of leaving this beautiful creature locked up in the cold, dank cellars of the dungeon below my castle. The dungeons haven't been used for many years since I typically have no need to take prisoners. My reputation as the Beast of Boding works pretty effectively at keeping trespassers and thieves at bay.

I breathe in the scent of Fiona's hair once again, and my chest tightens. Whatever fate sent her wandering onto my property, I find myself glad that she did. I've always led a lonely existence, but Fiona makes me long for more.

It's not just the fact that I lust for her with every fiber of my being, though when I realized she was spying on me earlier as I stroked myself to release, it took everything in me not to run over to her and mount her then and there. Still, knowing that she was watching me with those beautiful sapphire blue eyes all wide and inno-cent-looking had me coming harder than I've ever come before.

My need for this woman is like nothing I've ever known before, and while I want nothing more than to follow my primal instinct and mark her as mine, I gave her my word, and I intend to keep it. No matter how hard it may be. Literally.

She's silent and rigid as she lays in my arms, but eventually, the heat of my body lulls her into a relaxed state. I hear her breathing even out as she falls asleep, and then I'm free to gaze down at her all I want.

She's so tiny in my arms, and I gently brush her raven-colored hair back from her face. Her hair is soft and silky, and I marvel at the way it almost seems to glow with blue highlights in the candlelight.

Her cheeks are pink, and her little mouth is slightly parted in her sleep. Her dark eyelashes rest against her cheeks.

She looks so young and pure and perfect that I ache inside. She deserves so much better than to be kidnapped and locked away with a beast like me.

I know I should let her go, but my chest aches at the thought. Every muscle in my body tenses when I remember her speaking of marriage. I'll be damned if I sit back and watch her be married off. The thought of another man sheathing himself inside her wet heat or holding her in his arms makes me start losing control.

I take in a few deep breaths to keep myself from morphing into my animal state. I can't think of things that send me into a rage like that if I want to keep from scaring Fiona.

I'm a selfish creature, and I need to keep her here with me. It's no longer a matter of wanting. I feel like I'll die without her.

I stroke a tentative finger down her cheek. Her skin is the softest thing I've ever felt.

"Sleep, my pretty little raven-haired bird," I whisper as I continue to admire her.

My staff hasn't gone down since I've gotten her in my arms, but I'm not even concerned with that.

As much as I'm dying to bury myself inside what I already know will be a tight cunt, I'm also happy to just hold her like this.

My own little bird.

I don't know when I started referring to her as my little bird—only that it feels right.

And I have absolutely no plans of ever setting my little bird free. I'll keep her here in this gilded cage with me, and in time, she'll come to be content here.

That's what I tell myself anyway because it hurts too much to believe otherwise.

EIGHT

Fiona

I wake up to a band of iron wrapped around me. I blink blearily a couple of times before my eyes snap open when I realize what that band of iron is.

Broderick's arm.

I suddenly feel something else—something that feels like a rod of steel—poking against my behind. My mind is flooded with visions of Broderick stroking that rod of steel, and my face flushes.

Everything comes back to me in a rush then.

Him slinging me over his shoulder, carrying me to his room, and forcing me to sleep with him.

I'm surprised I was able to fall asleep at all and even more surprised that I just had the most restful sleep of my entire life wrapped up in his big arms.

"Good morning, little bird." I feel the rumble of his words go clean through me where my back is pressed against his chest.

I begin to wiggle to try to get away from him. He groans, his arm momentarily tightening against me. I think I feel him press that hardness deeper against me, but then he releases me, and I pop up out of the bed.

In my haste to get away from him, I've forgotten that I'm in a nearly see-through chemise, a fact that's made utterly visible when his eyes rake over my front and darken. He licks his lips, and I grab the bedding and pull it up to my chin.

In doing so, I strip it from him, and I'm suddenly staring right at the huge bulge of his hardness pressing against his breeches. I avert my eyes with a blush, and he chuckles before he gets out of bed and walks over to the wardrobe.

"There are clothes for you in that wardrobe

over there." He points to a wardrobe on the other side of the room.

I walk over to it, my eyes widening when I see all the dresses in it. I glance over at him quizzically.

"They were my mother's," he replies simply before he comes up behind me and selects a sapphire blue dress from the rack. "Wear this one. It matches your eyes."

His voice is husky, and it sends a shiver running through me. I consider denying his request because why should I do what he wants when he's holding me captive here?

But something about the fact that these dresses were his mother's and the way he says it has me unable to deny him.

I take the dress from him wordlessly and then wait for him to leave or at least turn around. When he makes no move to do either, I prompt him, "Do you mind?"

He blinks down at me before his mouth curves up into a wicked smile. Despite how big and growly he seems, he's actually quite handsome when he smiles. My heart skips a beat within me as I take in his smile.

"Not at all. By all means," he gestures with his

hand for me to go ahead, but he still makes no move to offer me any privacy.

"It's not proper for me to dress in front of you," I sputter.

His grin only widens. "We slept with our bodies molded together. I think we're beyond the bounds of propriety, little bird."

I scowl and hurry to dress as quickly as I can. I can feel his eyes on me the entire time. He has no shame.

And I can't help wondering if this is how it's always going to be. Am I just something to be on display for him? Is he going to just stare at me all the time? Will I never get another moment alone again?

I huff when I realize that I can't finish fastening the dress on my own. It has much more intricate closings than my simple dress, which is nowhere to be found. Belinda probably whisked it away to launder it, but when did she come collect it?

My face flushes anew when I think of her coming in and seeing me in bed with her master, though why I should care what his staff thinks is beyond me. All I should care about is getting out of here.

I feel Broderick right at my back, and then his fingers are deftly buttoning up the last closures on my dress.

I'm silent, my skin tingling at the slight sensation when his fingers brush my skin. When he's done, he takes my long hair in both of his hands and lifts it. I think he's sniffing it, and then I feel it drop down my back as he releases it.

He turns me then with his hands on my shoulders. I stare up into his stormy grey eyes and see the desire written plain as day on his face.

What's wrong with me that I feel an answering longing within my own body?

Just then, my stomach decides to rumble embarrassingly.

Broderick frowns. "Let's go feed you, little bird."

I frown back at him, offended at the way he talks about me like I'm some pet to take care of, and that's probably exactly what I am to him. Some amusement.

I cross my arms and glare up at him. "I'm not hungry," I lie.

"Don't be ridiculous, Fiona," he snaps at me. "I heard your stomach growl."

I shrug. "I'm fine." I'm not fine. I'm hungry and confused and irritated.

"Well, I'm hungry so accompany me to the dining room anyway," he grits out at me.

"I don't want to go anywhere with you," I spit back. "I'm your prisoner, and I refuse to trail behind you like a puppy dog."

Broderick's nostrils flare, and I take a step back, my eyes widening. I realize I might have gone too far with my defiance when I see his body beginning to sprout hair.

He growls and closes his eyes, taking in a few deep breaths before he relaxes, the hair retreating back into his body.

All I can do is stare at him in both amazement and trepidation.

"Do not ever refer to yourself as a dog in my presence again," he finally growls out.

I stare at him, shocked that that's what set him off. I figured he was mad about my defiance or my refusal to do everything he wants—not at the reference I made to him treating me like a pet.

"Why?" I ask him. "That's what you're treating me like. Some pet that you can feed and dress and order around. Is that why you brought me here?"

I might not have outright said it like I did the

first time, but apparently the message is still the same and Broderick was serious because he suddenly growls and his eyes glow silver. I watch as he morphs into his beastly form so fast I barely have time to process it.

He seems to grow even taller, and his entire body is covered in light brown fur. His eyes are still the same, though now they're blaring down at me in anger.

He takes a step toward me, and I stumble back a few steps, my entire body quaking with fear.

Why did part of me even want to see him in this state again? He's terrifying, and it's not his beastly form so much as the anger in his eyes that sends terror racing up my spine.

Why did I poke the bear? What the hell is wrong with me? I must have a death wish to keep underestimating Broderick.

I finally manage to get my wits about me enough to turn and take off running.

Away from Broderick.

Away from the Beast of Boding.

CHAPTER

NINE

Broderick

I snarl when I see Fiona running from me. I physically hold myself back from chasing after her. I know I could catch her within half a second, but I'm afraid that in my current state, I might grab her too harshly and hurt her.

I'm not always aware of my own strength, but especially so when I'm in my beastly state. I take in several deep breaths, trying to hold my beast at bay and make him recede back into me.

But it's all to no avail—especially when I hear

the slamming of my front door hitting the wall. Dammit! She's gotten out.

I go barreling through the corridors and out the front door. It's not so much that I fear her getting too far from me more so than I'm afraid she'll be hurt trying to navigate these woods that she's unfamiliar with. I know all too well the dangers that await a female out here all alone.

It's easy for me to track her. Her scent is so heavy in the air. I follow it like a trail of roses. Plus, I hear the crunch of the leaves and brush underfoot as she runs through the forest.

"Fiona!" I call out her name, but it comes out like a roar. I mentally curse myself when I realize this is no doubt only going to scare her even more.

My heart lurches in my chest, and I redouble my efforts when I hear her scream up ahead.

I'm upon her in an instant then, my every instinct roaring at me to get to her and protect her from whatever has hurt her.

She's laying on the ground, and panic seizes me at the sight of her still form. I drop to my knees beside her, and she moans.

I relax only the tiniest bit when I realize that she's still alive. My anger quickly fades to be replaced by concern for her welfare.

I feel myself morphing back down into my human state. I wait until the transformation is complete, and then I lean over her to inspect her injuries.

I touch her foot, and she winces as she cries out in pain.

A quick survey of her foot shows that it's her ankle. She's apparently twisted it.

My eyes canvas the area. I quickly spot the low-lying tree root she probably tripped over.

"Ssh," I try to soothe her as I scoop her up into my arms. "I've got you. It's okay." Of course, gauging by the way she just ran from me like the hounds of hell were nipping at her heels, that's probably not going to calm her any. My chest tightens within me. I hate the fact that she's so scared of me and so desperate to get away from me. I've never cared what any human thought of me before, but I care so much what Fiona thinks.

When she looks up and sees that I'm no longer in my beastly state, she seems to relax somewhat.

She lets out a tiny whimper before she buries her head in my chest. My chest swells with emotion at the action. No matter that she just ran from me. It's me she's seeking comfort from now.

I feel a pang when I'm reminded that she

wouldn't be hurt at all right now or need any sort of comfort had it not been for me to begin with.

Nevertheless, I stroke my hands down over her hair and her back, filled with remorse at scaring her so much that she ran from me.

I start carrying her back to my castle, the silence between us thick and heavy.

I finally speak the questions that are weighing on my mind, "Why did you run from me, Fiona? Don't you realize I would never hurt you? I just want to keep you." My voice comes out weary and resigned with my confession.

There's no use in pretending that I'm not the lonely, pathetic beast that I am—desperate enough to keep her against her will just so I'll have some company.

And the last thing I want is her pity, but her eyes seem to soften when she looks up at me. She stares at me for a moment before she finally admits, "It's true that you're scary when you're in your, uh..." she fumbles over the words before she finally settles on, "other form, but I think deep down, I do know that you would never really hurt me."

She looks down and licks her lips before

looking back up at me, her expression torn. It pierces my heart to see it. "It's my papa, Broderick. He already feels guilty about my mother's death, and I can't bear the thought of him worrying about what happened to me or feeling guilty. That's why I need to get back to him— to let him know that I'm okay." Her eyes are pleading, and I feel a new wave of guilt wash over me.

She has a family. She's not all alone like me. What right do I have to jerk her from her family and keep her here with me?

Yet, the thought of freeing her still causes that tight ache to form in my chest.

I'm still a selfish bastard. I guess I always will be.

But my mind casts about for a solution. A way that I can keep her while easing her fears and tempering her urge to run. I won't be able to live with myself if she keeps hurting herself by trying to escape me.

It suddenly comes to me. "How about we strike up a deal?"

She looks up at me, her eyes questioning.

"What kind of deal?" she asks cautiously.

I frown when I realize she probably thinks I'm going to barter for her physical body. I quickly turn my mind away from that thought before I become angered all over again.

I adjust her weight in my arms and hold her tighter against me.

"I'll let you send word to your father that you're okay." Her eyes widen. "In return," I go on, "you'll stop trying to run. You'll accept your life here."

Her eyes search mine hopefully, and then she bites her lips before murmuring to herself, "A willing prisoner, then."

I shrug. If that's how she needs to look at it in her mind to help her reconcile herself to it, then so be it.

"What do you have to lose?" I remind her. "You said your father is trying to marry you off to a man you don't want." I feel my entire body tense just at the thought. I inhale a deep breath. "If you stay here with me, I'll do everything I can to make you happy. Anything you want, just tell me and I'll get it. I don't want you to be miserable with me, Fiona," I confess. "I'd like you to be happy here." My voice is low as I bare my innermost thoughts as much as I dare to right now.

She's quiet as she contemplates my offer.

Thankfully she doesn't ask me why I want her to stay so badly.

I don't know what I would tell her if she did ask. Would I admit to her that I'm lonely? Would I admit to her that she's the most beautiful thing I've ever seen and I feel like I'll die without her?

I'm sure that wouldn't make sense to her. Hell, it doesn't even make sense to me. But it is what it is, and there's no changing it.

I've heard of shifters being predestined to a mate. I never thought that was in the cards for me, but maybe that's what's going on here. Maybe my beastly side recognizes her as my mate, and that's why I can't bear the thought of letting her go. It physically hurts me to think of never holding her in my arms like this again.

My hold tightens on her at the thought, pulling her closer against my chest.

Of course, she'll probably never want to mate with me, and I won't force her, but at least I can be near her, and that's something.

I meant what I said, too. I'll do anything in my power to make her happy.

Anything other than letting her go, that is.

I look back down at her, my eyes finding her sapphire blue ones.

"Well, what's it going to be, little bird?"

TEN

Fiona

My heart still gives this curious flutter when I remember the look of pleasant surprise on Broderick's face when I agreed to his deal.

It's like he halfway didn't expect me to. The obvious hope on his face when I agreed did funny things to my insides.

As much as I know I should hate Broderick, I just can't.

Yes, I realize that he kidnapped me and that in and of itself is criminal. However, at every turn, he's proving himself to be a decent human being.

He carried me all the way back to the castle, and he had my quarters moved to the room directly adjoining his. My face flamed at the sly look on Belinda's face when she confirmed that Broderick wanted me moved to the mistress' quarters. Apparently, the room I'm now occupying was where his mother used to stay, while Broderick stays in the master's quarters, which were previously his father's. I know how that probably looks to his staff, and I'm sure the tongues have been wagging, but there's not really anything I can do about it, so I've decided that I'm not going to care.

Once we returned back to the castle after my mishap, Broderick laid me gently on the bed and tended to my injured foot himself. Thankfully, it didn't appear I broke it. I just strained it, which means that I have to pretty much stay off of it for a while.

And that's something that Broderick is certainly holding me to. He's hovering over me like an overprotective parent. If I ever make any move to try to get up on my own, he's right there scooping me up into his arms to carry me wherever I want to go.

It's frustrating, yet it's kind of sweet at the same time. He truly is worried about me.

He's apologized to me a thousand times over for scaring me and swears that even when his anger becomes so uncontrollable that he can't help but morph into his beastly state that I never need to worry—that even in that state he would never hurt me.

And I tend to believe him. That still doesn't mean that if he morphs into that state again, I won't be frightened out of my wits, because it's truly a terrifying thing to see. And like I said before, it's not the beastly look of him that's so terrifying so much as the furious look in his eyes.

I learned from Belinda that Broderick is the result of a full-blooded shifter father and half-shifter mother. His father was a purebred bear shifter, but his mother was half human, half wolf shifter, which is why Broderick's animal resembles a beast that's half wolf, half bear.

And Broderick was as good as his word. Once we reached the castle, he fetched a piece of parchment and a quill and let me pen a letter to my father in my own hand.

Knowing that Broderick would read the letter, I didn't give any indication of my whereabouts or what had happened to me. I merely kept it brief, telling him that I was okay but that I would likely never return and for him to not worry. He'll have questions, but at least this way, he'll know that I'm alive and well—at least I hope he'll believe I'm well.

Broderick scanned the contents of the letter before he let out a grunt of approval and called for one of his servants to deliver it to the address I gave him.

So, Broderick held up his end of the bargain.

And now it's my turn to hold up mine. No more escape attempts. I'm simply to submit to my new life here.

Honestly, it's kind of a relief to have the decision taken from me like that. It gives me a sense of freedom I've never felt before. I feel like now I'm allowed to relax and try to enjoy myself here because this is where I'm going to be for the rest of my life.

I no longer have to feel guilty about liking anything about this place because I'm supposed to be resigned to being here now.

It's ironic that I'm finding freedom in my captivity, yet there it is.

Now that I've agreed not to try to escape, Broderick no longer has a need to make me sleep with him every night. However, that doesn't stop him from coming into my room at night and helping me undress before scooping me up into his arms and carrying me into his quarters.

The first night when he walked wordlessly into my room and collected me, I followed his lead and remained silent and unresisting. I've never protested when he does it. I've always just let him carry me there and curl his big body around me—my back to his front.

If I'm being totally honest, I've come to like the feeling of being held in his arms all night.

And true to his word, he's never tried anything. I always feel that hardness pressing into me, but that's it.

Not once has he tried to take my virginity or force me to do anything.

Also true to his word, Broderick gets me anything I ask for, any type of food or book or anything.

Of course, I don't ask for much. Broderick's library already has so many books that it'll take me three lifetimes to read all the tomes in it as it is.

I'm no longer plotting any escapes, so I don't sass back at him or argue with him. There's no longer that thought that I must try to pull back from him and get away from him. Therefore, I haven't angered him enough to see him morph into his beastly state again.

In fact, I've actually found him to be a very amicable person to be around. Broderick is very well-read and smart. He's read way more about physics and science than I have, and he can hold his own in conversation on any topic. He's actually a genius, and we spend many afternoons sitting together silently by the fire and reading our respective tomes. Then we discuss what we read over dinner.

We've kind of fallen into a little routine. We get up, and Broderick takes me outside and sets me on a bench where I watch him tend to his garden. He educates me on the different types of flora and how to care for them, promising to teach me anything I want to know. His eyes light up when I show interest and ask questions, and he's actually a very competent teacher. I feel like I've learned a lot just listening to him talk about his hobbies and things he's read. I can't help thinking that he'd be a wonderful father someday.

I blush even thinking that, though, because then that makes me think of the hardness between his legs and *how* babies are made. I know that Broderick desires me. It's obvious, yet he's been more of a gentleman than many of the men in town who label themselves as such. I know Broderick wants me physically, yet he also seems just as content just to be in my company.

That doesn't mean he doesn't take any excuse he can to touch me, though.

After Broderick's done in the garden, we usually go for a walk around the property. Well, Broderick walks while he carries me. I honestly suspect that I'm more than capable of putting weight on my foot again, but I think he just wants an excuse to carry me around everywhere.

And while I've actually become accustomed to how good it feels to be in his arms, I know that I've got to start using my foot again if I ever want it to heal properly. Gently pointing that out to Broderick is the only thing that has him allowing me to take a few measured steps on my own—with him hovering right by my side to catch me in case I stumble or fall of course.

Sometimes, he has Belinda prepare us a picnic, and we have it out on the grounds under a willow tree or by the creek running across this property. Other times, like when it's raining, we picnic on the library floor in front of a crackling fire.

As the days pass on, I become more and more

comfortable at Broderick's castle. I realize that I probably have a much better life here than I ever would have had had I gone back to my father. I feel guilty for admitting that, but if I'd been successful in my escape and made it back to him, I'd probably be married off to that odious old toad, Lord Fairchild by now.

At least with Broderick, I have a gentle companion—one who will do anything to make me happy.

It sounds crazy to admit, but I'm happier here with the Beast of Boding than I've ever been.

In fact, being with him feels like home.

Broderick

It becomes harder and harder to be around Fiona every day and not claim her as my mate. The more I'm around her, the more my body recognizes her as my mate. I'm as sure of this as I am that the sun will rise in the morning.

It's becoming increasingly difficult to fight those primal urges that keep welling up within me. I don't only want to thrust up into her and claim her innocence for my own, but I want to bite her neck and leave my mark and scent all on her.

Stroking myself to release in a private bath every day isn't cutting it. All it takes is one more waft of her scent, one more glimpse of her sweet, ripe, lush young body and I'm aching with need again no matter how much I've released.

It's more than the physical aspect too. I'm already around her nearly every minute of every hour of the day, but those few minutes that we spend apart bathing in our separate chambers are torturous for me. I need to have her near me at all times.

I'd love nothing more than to have her in my steaming tub with me and watch the water flow over her naked skin. I long to lather up her hair and wash it for her. I want to rub oils on her skin for her.

I just want her near me. Always. The beast within me brays every second we're parted. My need for her is verging on obsession, but I can't help it. I can't stop it any more than I can stop the tide from breaking.

It's truly torturous for me to sleep with her body pressed against me all night, but I can't bring myself to let her sleep in a separate room from me. I'd rather torture myself and have her in my arms than go through the torture of not having her here.

I never truly realized just how dark and bleak my existence was before I brought her here. She's like a shining light, her laughter and smile bringing joy to my every day.

I'm holding her in my arms now, stroking my hands over her raven-colored hair as she sleeps. She's so beautiful in her slumber, so sweet and innocent looking. I usually stay awake for an hour or two every night just watching her before I allow myself to go to sleep. I cherish these moments to hold her while she sleeps, to watch over her, my eyes drinking her in greedily.

This is what is sustaining me right here. I tell myself every day that this is enough.

I almost manage to convince myself of it when she mumbles in her sleep. I crane my head down closer to hear her, and then I realize that it's my name she's moaning.

"Broderick, Broderick," she's moaning in a breathy little voice over and over again. Her skin looks flushed, and I smell the scent of her arousal permeating through the bedding.

All my instincts flare to life. I grit my teeth and try to fight against the urges suddenly rushing through my body. My cock is at full mast pressing against her ass, seeking entry into that sweet, dripping hole. The knowledge that it's me she's dreaming about, that it's me that has her body so worked up, is almost enough to send me over the edge

"Broderick," she moans my name again, her body pressing against me. Her scent is assaulting my nostrils. She smells like honey, and my mouth begins watering for a taste. I have to find out if she's as sweet as she smells.

I begin moving my hand down her stomach and then up her leg below her chemise until my hand meets the wetness between her thighs.

She moans when my fingers touch her, and I let out a moan of my own. She thrusts her hips up into my hand.

I look down at her. Her eyes are still closed, and her lips are parted sweetly, still in sleep.

She might be a virgin, but she's a horny little virgin, and her body knows exactly what to do.

Her little hips are humping up into my fingers, seeking the friction she needs.

"Broderick," she moans my name again and whimpers. That whimper sends a rush of possessive masculinity coursing through my veins, and that's when I snap.

I can't take it anymore. I climb down the bed and position myself between her sweet thighs.

I don't know if it's my sudden movement or something else, but her eyes suddenly flutter open. They're still glazed with the lust of whatever she was dreaming, though. She looks at me kneeling between her thighs, and her eyes widen as she begins to come to herself. "What are you—" her voice comes out breathy, but I interrupt her.

"Just a taste, Fiona. Just one taste. That's all I'm asking. That's all I need, little bird." My voice is a desperate plea, and I don't wait for her answer, afraid that she'll turn me down in virgin shyness.

I plunge my head between her legs, my tongue instantly snaking out to lave her from slit to clit. She jerks when my tongue hits that bundle of nerves at the top of her mound.

I repeat the motion over and over again, lapping up more of her sugary sweet cream with each pass of my tongue.

Mine, mine, mine. The thought is reverberating throughout my head like a heartbeat. *My mate.* If there was ever any doubt in my head before, there's none now. Fiona is my mate. Nothing has ever tasted so right on my tongue.

When her little hands fist in my hair as I continue to lap at her, I'm suddenly filled with such a rush of love so potent that it almost makes me dizzy.

It suddenly clicks within me. I love her. I love this beautiful little woman more than life itself. *My Fiona. Mine.*

I focus all my attention on her little swollen pearl, swirling my tongue around it and sucking it in my mouth until she's writhing with pleasure and begging incoherently, her voice so beautiful.

My cock is so swollen I'm leaking and leaving a wet spot in my breeches, but I ignore the raging monster between my legs demanding attention. Her pleasure is more important to me right now.

"Broderick," she pants out, "I—I—something is...Oh my—!" she trails off with a scream, and then I feel her body explode underneath me.

Her wetness gushes onto my face, and I lap it up like the hungry beast I am. I continue to gently lick and suck her as she comes down from her orgasm. I don't stop until I feel her body go lax in my hold.

Only then do I climb back up to settle myself back beside her, ignoring my aching staff as I pull her into my arms. No sooner do I get her there than she's already drifting back off to sleep.

I plant a kiss on her forehead, my heart heavy with my newfound realization and the knowledge of what I must do with it.

CHAPTER

TWELVE

Fiona

For the first time since he's brought me to this castle, Broderick isn't there holding me when I awaken.

I awaken slowly, blinking to clear the sleep from my eyes. I stretch as I remember having the most amazing dream. Broderick was kissing me all over. His lips were on my lips, my neck, my shoulders, my arms. My skin felt like it was on fire, and wetness pooled in between my thighs. There was an insistent throbbing there too, an ache that only he could fill.

I remember how silvery gray his eyes looked in my dream and how his brown hair fell about his face wildly, making him look so rugged and untamed, his chiseled jawline handsome and proud.

Suddenly, I straighten and my eyes snap open when I realize that it wasn't all a dream. I'd woken up to find Broderick between my legs as if he'd just been continuing my dream in real life because right before I awoke, my dream Broderick had been kissing my bare stomach.

My face flushes when I remember the pleasure his mouth gave me. Broderick has never even kissed my lips, yet he kissed me in the most intimate of places, and it felt so good. I didn't even know you could be kissed down *there*. The little snaps and crackles of pleasure that had buzzed through me were beyond anything I could have ever imagined.

And when the pressure within me had built and then spilled over...I honestly didn't know women could experience such pleasure. It's always been my understanding that sex is usually just pleasurable for the man. Of course, it's not like I have a mother to explain things to me, and my father has certainly never broached the subject with me. What little I know about the sexual act was all gleaned from Greta. Maybe she'd only been speaking to her experience, and if that's true, a wave of sympathy goes through me that she never experienced the kind of pleasure Broderick gave me last night.

I start wondering if men can receive pleasure in the same way. My face blushes even hotter at the thought.

My cheeks pinken further when I realize that I fell asleep on him. I don't know if we'd have actually coupled last night or not, but Broderick was surely left wanting when I passed out on him. Is that normal? For women to experience such intense pleasure that they pass out?

I have so many questions and no one to ask other than Broderick, and I'm filled with embarrassment at the thought of voicing those questions aloud to him.

I wonder where he went. It's not like him to leave me alone for very long, even though I can completely walk on my own now. He hasn't been carrying me around as much lately, but that's at my instance and none of his own. Sometimes I still see his arms twitching at his sides like he's fighting back the urge to pick me up.

I get up and get dressed in one of the blue dresses that Broderick loves. He loves me in blue. It's his favorite color on me. He says it brings out the sapphire blue of my eyes, and suddenly I want nothing more than to please him.

I hurry outside anxiously, heading to the garden, figuring that's where I'll find him since that's usually where we are at this time of morning. I frown when I don't see him bent over his plants. I head into the library, but I don't find him there either.

I wander around the castle, aimlessly looking for him, wondering where he could be. And then I finally come across his study. Broderick is very rarely in there, but I push open the door anyway, wondering if maybe that's where he is this morning. Maybe that's why he left me all alone. He had some business to attend to or something.

My heart leaps up into my chest when I crack the door open and see his big frame standing in front of the window, looking out across his grounds.

"Good morning, Broderick," I tell him shyly, suddenly nervous around him after last night.

"Fiona," he says my name stiffly and doesn't turn around to look at me.

My face falls. Why is he so aloof? Is this about last night? Is he disappointed in me? Was my response to him not normal?

He still doesn't turn around to look at me.

"Is something wrong?" I ask him hesitantly. I don't know why, but I sense that something is off today.

He doesn't answer me for a long while, but when he does, what he says couldn't shock me any more than if he told me pigs fly.

"I'm letting you go, Fiona." His voice is harsh.

I grab onto the edge of the chair back to keep myself from falling over, my heart thundering rapidly inside my chest. Did I hear him right?

"Wha—what?" I stammer.

"You're free to go," he repeats, his voice flat and cold.

I just stand there mutely. I should be rejoicing. He's giving me my freedom. I can go home to my father. I'm no longer a prisoner.

Yet why do I feel no joy? Why do I feel this hard little pit in my stomach?

I stand there dumbly, unable to move or form words. The silence stretches between us, though he still makes no move to turn around and look at me.

"Did you hear me?" he finally growls, his voice harsh. "I said you can go home now. I'm no longer keeping you prisoner."

My brow furrows in confusion, I feel that falling sensation in my stomach. I feel like I might be sick. How can he send me away after last night?

A rumbling sound unlike any I've ever heard bursts from his chest. I watch with wide eyes as he morphs into his beastly form, gasping when he turns around to face me.

He stands tall and proud, his eyes blazing down at me.

I don't run from him this time, though. Instead, I stand here taking in every bit of his beast with my eyes. I know he won't hurt me.

He looks confused that I'm not running. I take a step toward him, drawn inexplicably to him. I want to touch his fur and feel it beneath my fingertips.

His eyes widen and he growls in warning as he's the one who takes a step back from me this time. I stop and hold my breath like someone who's approaching a wild animal.

"Fiona, go" his voice is a low growl.

I start to shake my head and protest, but then he roars, "Go, Fiona! Now!"

Something in his tone brooks no argument, and I realize that he's deathly serious. He wants me to leave.

Tears prick my eyes as the betrayal knifes at my chest.

He's sending me away. All I can think is that what happened between us last night displeased him.

My face flames with hurt and humiliation as I finally turn on my heels and run, except this time I'm not running from him in fear. This time, I'm running because he told me to.

THIRTEEN

Broderick

I'm miserable. It feels like a part of me has been ripped violently away from my body.

It's more than an emotional ache. It's a physical ache not having Fiona here with me.

I guess what they say about fated mates is true. You truly do feel like you'll die without your other half near you.

She's fine without me, though. I assure myself of that. She doesn't have the beastly side to her that I do, so she doesn't feel this primal pull. In fact, she's probably relieved to be back home with her father. Back where she really belongs.

She really belongs here with us, my beast snarls at me in my head, cursing at me and calling me every type of fool in the book for letting her go.

He selfishly wanted to keep her here with us, but my human side told me that if I really loved her, I couldn't keep her captive. I can't expect her to return my feelings of love. Not whenever we started off the way we did with me kidnapping her. Any feelings that she would ever grow to have for me would always be rooted in the falsehood of our beginning.

Sure, she might come to care for me in time, but it would only be because I'm the only person she's around. Not because she truly cares about me of her own accord, and while my beast says that we can deal with that, that we'll take her any way we can, my human side tells me that it's morally wrong, that if I really love her, I will set her free to make her own decisions.

I ran for days in my beastly form, picking fights with every predator in the forest. Anything to help me try to forget the pain of living without her.

I come limping back into my castle, my fur wet

and sodden. Only when I'm inside do I allow myself to morph back into my human form.

Belinda greets me at the door, her eyes full of pity, but thankfully, she doesn't offer any empty platitudes. I think my housekeeper is wiser than she lets on. She knows what Fiona is to me. She knows what I've lost.

My housekeeper just draws me a bath. She has food prepared for me, but even the scent of my favorite dishes wafting up to me isn't enough to entice me to leave my room and eat.

Instead, I soak in the water, aching inside. I wish I could feel numb. I'd rather not feel anything than feel this twisting, tormenting ache in the void where my little bird should be.

Fiona's scent still permeates my bed, so I crawl in it and inhale deeply, my soul aching for her.

My beast is telling me to go out and get her, to bring her back to us. But my human side is just as stubborn as my beastly side and resists, telling myself that I did the right thing.

I didn't want to let her go, but I had to because that one taste was enough to let me know just what she meant to me.

And I know beyond a shadow of a doubt if I ever take her, then there's no way I'll ever be able to let her go. My desire for her is too strong already. I don't think I could have spent another day with her without claiming her as my own.

No, it's best for me to cut ties with her now before it becomes even more difficult to do so—no matter how much it's tearing me up inside.

Because Fiona deserves much better than me.

Fiona

I finger the amulet at my throat and gaze out into the forest in the direction of Broderick's castle.

I wonder what he's doing right now. If I were there, we would probably be in the library right about now sitting in companionable silence in front of the roaring fire and reading our respective books. Then we'd head to the dining hall for dinner and talk about everything we'd read.

My heart aches at the memory. I still can't believe he sent me away after how adamant he was about keeping me. We made the deal that I would stay with him forever if he would just let me send word to my father that I was okay. I never dreamed he would be the one to change his mind.

The irony that I'm longing to be back with him after I'd wanted my freedom so viciously in the beginning isn't lost on me. I should be glad that he let me go home to my papa.

And I was glad to see papa again. He hugged me so tight I'm surprised he didn't crack one of my ribs.

I feel guilty for longing to go back to Broderick when I recall the tears of relief in my father's eyes upon seeing me stumble through the woods back up to our little cottage.

Papa has asked me repeatedly where I was when I was away, but I've refused to tell him. For some reason, it feels like betraying Broderick to tell him, and I don't want to put Broderick in any sort of danger.

That's crazy, too. I'm trying to protect my kidnapper. I should be telling everyone what he did to me so that the townspeople can storm his gates and make him pay for his crimes.

Yet I don't. I don't want anything to happen to Broderick. In fact, I wish I was back there with him now.

I sigh.

"I know where you were, Fi." Papa's quiet voice surprises me. He comes up on my left and sits on the old fallen log I'm sitting on gazing toward Broderick's castle.

I glance over at him but don't speak.

"You've been staring in the direction of Broderick Boding's castle every day ever since you got back."

My heart leaps up into my chest and I sit up straighter, my eyes going wide as I look over at my papa. How does he always seem to know what's wrong with me even without me telling him? He's always been that way.

He gives me a knowing look. "I know the look of a woman in love," he says gently. "Your mother used to have the same look on her face when she looked at me." He smiles sadly.

He levels me with a questioning look. "But what I don't understand is why you came back if you love this man."

I don't answer. My throat feels tight, and I feel tears welling up in my eyes.

He shakes his head slowly before he finally says, "I can't believe my daughter is in love with the Beast of Boding."

I immediately jump to Broderick's defense. "He's not a beast, Papa. Well, I mean he is. He's a shifter. He turns into an animal form that looks something like a bear or wolf, but he's more human than most men I've ever met! Yes, he has a temper, but he's really very gentle and..." I trail off when I see the soft smile playing on my father's lips.

"I believe you, sweetheart. I don't believe a bad man could have captured my daughter's heart."

"What I'd like to know is how you ended up meeting him."

"Well, he actually kidnapped me." I decide to tell my papa the truth.

"You were kidnapped by the Beast of Boding?" my father asks, the alarm in his voice evident. "The Beast of Boding," a shocked voice sounds from behind us.

We both turn around to see Lord Fairchild standing there.

Dread settles in the pit of my stomach when I see the look written on Lord Fairchild's face. He's not going to let this go. He's going to raise a mob against Broderick.

I rush to assure him, "I'm fine, Lord Fairchild. The beast didn't hurt me."

Lord Fairchild snorts, his jowls jiggling with the movement. "Of course, he did. He's a beast."

My papa stands up to intervene, but Lord Fairchild starts speaking again before my father can utter a good—what good it would do anyway.

"Don't worry, Fiona," Lord Fairchild assures me. "I'll make sure the beast pays for this," he vows before he turns without another word and heads off.

I cast a panicked look at my father, and he nods at me. "Go Fiona. I understand. Do what you must."

Papa hugs me to him tightly and places a kiss on my cheek before I take off running into the forest toward Broderick's castle.

FOURTEEN

Broderick

"Broderick! Broderick!"

I miss Fiona so much I must have slipped into a state of delirium. I'm hearing her voice calling out my name inside my head.

I hear my name a couple more times, only this time they sound louder and closer. I stop mid-stride and crane my head toward the sound.

There it is again. I'm not imagining things. Fiona is really out there in the woods, and she's calling my name.

Her voice sounds desperate, and my chest tightens in response. Is she in trouble?

I follow the sound of her voice, her scent getting stronger the closer I get to her.

I inhale deeply, filling my lungs with as much of it as I can. Fuck, how I've missed the scent of her.

"Fiona?" I call out.

"Broderick!" Her voice sounds relieved, and then I see her up ahead. I break out into a run to get to her.

"What's wrong, little bird? Are you hurt? Are you in trouble?" I hold her at arm's length, looking her up and down. My fingertips are buzzing at the contact where they grip her arms.

She shakes her head, and my eyes are drawn to a blue stone glowing about her throat. Before I have a chance to ask her about it, she answers me, "No, no, I'm fine, but you're not, Broderick."

My eyes snap back up to hers, and my heart begins to beat faster in my chest at the concern I see in her eyes—concern for *me*.

But she's way off base. I don't know what she's got cooked up in that little head of hers, but there's no way I'm the one in danger. I'm a predator more than capable of defending myself.

"What are you talking about, Fiona?" I ask her gently. "Moreover, what are you doing out here in these woods all by yourself?" I scowl down at her. Doesn't she realize the danger in these woods? Anything could have happened to her.

She ignores my second question. "It's Lord Fairchild. He's raising a mob to come out here after you." She bites her lip guiltily then. "He overheard me talking to my father, and he got the wrong idea. He thinks you've wronged me, and he intends to make you pay for it."

Anger blooms in my chest at hearing another man's name come from her lips. "Is this Fairchild your intended?" My vision starts bleeding red at the thought, and I feel myself beginning to morph. I fight for control of my beast, only gaining a modicum of it back when Fiona shakes her head.

"He wants to be, but my papa knows my heart lies elsewhere."

She's blushing now, and I look down at her incredulously as the meaning of what she's saying begins to dawn on me.

"Fiona, I—" my tongue feels thick, my throat clogged with emotion. I can't form the words to express what I'm feeling. My chest is so tight I feel like I might burst.

She misinterprets my speechlessness. "It's okay," she stammers. "I know you don't feel the same way. I figured out that's why you sent me away, but I had to warn you they were coming." Those sapphire blue eyes are shimmering blue pools when she turns them up at me again.

I'm still speechless. I can't believe this beautiful woman thinks I don't want her. "Fiona," I try again, and my voice works this time, though it comes out rough and gravelly, "I didn't send you away because I didn't want you." I let out a half-choked laugh at the thought. "I sent you away because I want you *too* much."

Her little brow furrows like she doesn't understand my meaning.

I let out an incredulous chuckle. All this time, my little bird has been longing to return to her cage. "As much as I loved having you with me, it was becoming more difficult for me to control myself around you. That last night was evidence of that." My eyes glaze over at the memory, my cock stiffening in my breeches even now. "If you only knew how close I came to taking you that night."

I shake my head, my hands fisting on her shoulders. I release my hold on her, not wanting to hurt her in my passion. "I had to let you go to protect you from me. I couldn't risk hurting you. I'd have taken you against your will eventually. See, my beast," my voice becomes huskier with my admission, "he recognizes you as his mate. It's not uncommon for shifters to have a fated mate. I never dreamed I would have one until I met you. But you're a human, and I realize you don't feel the same—"

"I do!" she blurts, cutting me off. I stare down at her wide eyes, hardly able to believe my ears. "I do feel it," she continues, her face flushed prettily. "I was always drawn to you, even when I was a bit terrified of you, and ever since you sent me away, it's like..." she fumbles over her words.

"Like a piece of you is missing?" I supply, taking a step toward her, my chest swelling with emotion.

She looks up at me with wide eyes, nodding her head. "Exactly. All I've thought about is getting back to you, but I couldn't bear the thought of you rejecting me again." Her face falls at the memory, and I can bear it no longer.

I pull her flush against my chest, my beast roaring in triumph at finally having her back in our arms. "I didn't reject you, Fiona. Never, never, would I do that. I want you more than I want my next breath. I didn't think you wanted *me*. I kept you prisoner. I used your love for your father as a bargaining chip. How can you forgive me for my crimes?" Shame colors my voice. "This Fairchild, he's right. I have wronged you."

She presses herself closer against me. "No, you haven't! I wouldn't change a thing about how we met, Broderick. I'll gladly be your prisoner all over again."

I cup her face in one of my big hands, marveling at how tiny she is in my hold. "Not my prisoner," I assure her. "My mate."

Her breath catches, and my eyes are drawn down to those puffy pink lips. I wonder if they taste just as sweet as her other lips. My cock begins leaking at the memory. I haven't touched myself since the day she left. I couldn't bring myself to pleasure myself that way. It hurt too much to think about her knowing that she was gone.

My balls are so heavy with seed they must weigh ten pounds each. I'm aching and so overfull that the slightest friction will probably have me flooding my breeches.

But I ignore my cock's needs, the need to finally taste my mate's kiss even greater. I begin moving my head down toward hers, my lips already tingling in anticipation of meeting hers.

Her breath comes in shallow pants the closer I get to her, and I feel her little hands digging into my chest where she's gripping me.

Before my lips ever touch hers, though, there's a cry from right behind us.

"Unhand her, Beast!"

Fiona

Broderick's lip curls up into a snarl, and his eyes take on that silvery glow as he moves to stand in front of me, pushing me protectively behind him.

He's not even morphed into his beastly form yet, yet he's never seemed more animalistic than in this moment when he's guarding me predatorily.

And I feel completely safe with him. I know he won't let anything happen to me.

My eyes scan the perimeter, and I'm relieved to see that there's no one with Lord Fairchild.

However, that doesn't mean that more people aren't on their way—a fact that's proven true when I see the forms beginning to emerge from the trees up ahead.

My heart begins to hammer within my chest. I know Broderick's strong, and there's no doubt he could take Lord Fairchild in combat, but can he withstand so many without being harmed?

"Broderick..." my voice is shaky with panic, but Broderick merely reaches behind and lays a comforting hand on my arm.

"It's okay, Fiona. Trust me. No one will take you from me."

I feel a rush of calm spread through me at both his touch and the reassuring confidence of his tone, though that's not what I'm afraid of. I believe he'd die before letting anyone part us. No, what I fear is him getting hurt.

Lord Fairchild half turns to the mob of people forming behind him, his eyes never leaving Broderick as he draws his sword. "See how this beast has stolen our fair maiden away from us! He has his dirty paws all over her as we speak!"

The crowd roars, and Broderick snarls. I can tell he's fighting to keep his beast contained.

Lord Fairchild makes a lunge around Broderick

as if to go for me. I cower closer to Broderick's back, and that's when it happens.

I feel the fur sprouting beneath my fingers where I'm clutching onto Broderick's back. He literally morphs right underneath my fingertips, and I marvel at how soft his fur is.

I hear the collective gasp of all the towns-people and Lord Fairchild's voice rising above them all, "Beast!"

The throng begins moving closer to us, and Broderick roars. They stop for a moment before they begin moving in again, murder in their eyes.

"No!" I suddenly thrust myself in front of Broderick and splay my hands on either side of me. It's not like I'm really big enough to cover him, but my display of protection has the desired effect. Everyone halts in their tracks.

"He didn't hurt me!" I plead with the crowd.

Lord Fairchild scoffs much like he did when he overheard me and my father talking. "He's obvi-ously bewitched her. She doesn't know what she's saying."

I scowl at him. "I most certainly do, and he's a shifter—not a warlock!"

I hear the surprised murmurs go through the crowd. We've all heard of shifters before, but few have seen them. They've become a dying breed. At that word, the crowd seems to regard Broderick more with curiosity than anything else.

Lord Fairchild steps up and addresses the crowd again, "Regardless of what he is, he still kidnapped our poor Fiona here."

A few murmurs go through the crowd.

Broderick growls when I step forward. This time, it's me who reaches back a reassuring hand to pat his fur.

I feel his body calm under my touch much like mine did his.

"Broderick would never hurt me!" I tell the crowd. "In fact, we're fated mates."

The clearing goes so quiet that you can hear the softest rustle of the leaves from a squirrel skittering across them.

There are more murmurs from the crowd before someone finally points at me. "Look, her amulet. It's glowing!"

Everyone knows the story of the amulet my mother gave me and how it will glow when I'm in the presence of my true love, and they also believe in its power since they witnessed it firsthand. My mother used to wear the amulet herself, and it always glowed in the presence of my father and no other.

I look down. I can't see the amulet since it's close about my neck in a choker style, but I can see the glow illuminating my skin.

My heart begins a wild gallop in my chest. I've despaired of ever seeing the amulet glow, and now here it is. If I needed any further proof about my feelings for Broderick or what we are to one another, this just highlights the truth I already feel in my soul.

Broderick really is my one true love, my fated mate.

I laugh to myself as I realize if only I'd been wearing the amulet the day we'd met, we might have saved each other a lot of time and misunderstanding because the amulet doesn't lie. I'd have known the moment I saw it glowing that what it decreed was fate and couldn't be changed. Maybe then I'd have accepted everything between us more readily.

"It really is fate," I hear another voice say.

"The amulet doesn't lie!" another voice chimes in.

Before I know it, the townspeople are congratulating us instead of trying to murder Broderick.

Lord Fairchild is sputtering his indignation, but no one is paying him any mind.

I feel Broderick's entire body calm and relax, and I sense rather than see his transition back to his human state behind me.

The crowd oohs and aahs as they witness it, and I turn around to look at my mate. He's ignoring the crowd. He only has eyes for me.

"Did you mean what you said, little bird, or were you only trying to save my ass?" his gruff voice demands.

I feel my face flush, but I look him straight in the eyes as I confess, "I meant every word." I finger the amulet at my throat. "And the amulet really doesn't lie. My mother always told me it would glow when I'm in the presence of my true love, and well..." I trail off, looking up at him and biting my lip.

He groans, his eyes flicking to my lips before he looks up at our audience and frowns. He lifts his head and addresses the crowd, "Now that you see all is well, I'll be taking my mate home with me."

He doesn't wait for their assent. He scoops me up into his arms effortlessly and cradles me against his chest before he begins stomping through the woods toward his castle.

I can't stop the smile that plays at the corner of my lips.

He looks down at me with a raised eyebrow. "What's so funny, little bird?"

I giggle. "I can't help but feel like we've been here before."

His own lips twitch as he continues hauling me to his castle. Once the gray stones come into view, a peace settles over me. What I once thought looked so dark and foreboding fills my spirit with light and happiness.

Home. Broderick has brought me home.

No. I look up at my fated mate's handsome face. It's not the castle that's home.

It's him. Broderick. He's my home. As long as I'm with him, I'll be home.

SIXTEEN

Broderick

I can't wait to get her inside my castle's walls. I've been tromping through the forest with a painfully hard erection. I'm so swollen with need that a steady stream of liquid is leaking from my tip.

Every atom in my body is demanding I finally claim my mate as mine, and that's what I intend to do.

"Master Boding!" Belinda exclaims with a squeal that seems too girlish for her advanced age when I burst through the front door with Fiona in my arms. "Mistress Fiona!"

Fiona gives her a little wave, but I never stop in my journey toward the bedroom. "There will be time to catch up later, Belinda. For now, see that we're not disturbed."

I catch the twinkle in my housekeeper's eyes as she smiles and nods her head. "Would you like me to make up a room for your guest?"

"No!" I bark out before I turn my eyes back to Fiona. "She'll be staying with me." Her breath catches, and her cheeks blush prettily.

I'm going to have her blushing everywhere in a few minutes.

No sooner do I kick the door to my bedroom shut do I finally allow my lips to descend on hers. I've been dying to take them, but I didn't want our first kiss to have an audience. I wanted her all to myself when I tasted her for the first time.

And fuck me, but she tastes incredible. Her mouth is like nectar from the gods. She's so sweet it hurts, and the way she moves her little tongue against mine, meeting me stroke for stroke, has all the blood in my body rushing south straight to my cock.

"Fiona, my love, my mate, I need you," I breathe against her lips.

"I need you too, Broderick." Her sweet breath

fans over my lips, nearly driving me insane. Hell, everything about her drives me crazy, and I haven't even gotten her naked yet.

She runs her hands up my chest, and tingles shoot throughout my entire body. I groan and grab her hands, my own shaking with my passion.

"How fond are you of this dress?" I ask her.

She looks up at me quizzically. "It's just an old day dress."

Once I find out it wasn't her mother's and doesn't have any sentimental value, I rip it clean down the middle, ripping the shift underneath it as well. I'll buy her a hundred more dresses and shifts. I need to see her bare skin. Now.

She gasps as she looks up at me with wide eyes. I would think I've frightened her, but I see the way she clenches her thighs together.

Fuck, she wants this. I smell the thick scent of her arousal, and it's so intoxicating, I sway on my feet with lust.

I rip my shirt and breeches from my own body, and I see her eyes widen as she takes in my thick girth and long length. I'm aware that I'm larger than a normal human, but I frame her face with my hands and force her to meet my eyes. "It'll fit, little bird. I promise," I seek to reassure her. "There will be some pain, but I vow to you that I'll make it all worth it. I'll give you more pleasure than you've ever known."

She bites her lip and nods up at me, and that trust is everything. I feel the weight of responsibility settle on my shoulders, and I know that I will do everything in my power to make sure she gets just as much pleasure from our coupling as I do.

I drop my lips to hers again and rejoice in the way I feel her body melt into mine at my kiss. Her little breasts are pressed against me, and my hard shaft is cradled against her stomach. I can't help it and rut against her, leaving a trail of wetness in my wake before I finally force myself to stop and lift her into my arms.

I carry her over to the bed and lay her gently on it.

She looks so beautiful with her dark hair fanned out around her and her blue eyes shimmering up at me in the candlelight.

She holds her arms to me with a blush and a shy smile, and who I am to deny her invitation?

I eagerly enter her embrace, loving the feeling of her tiny arms attempting to wrap around me.

She can't even get them halfway around me. I'm so big compared to her.

I settle between her legs, my swollen shaft prodding her wet hole. I don't enter her right away, though. I lean down and kiss her neck, her shoulders, her breasts. I worship her, my tongue gliding over her porcelain skin, taking pleasure in every gasp and sigh that comes from her sweet lips.

"Broderick, please," she finally whispers. "I want to feel you inside me. Claim me. Make me yours."

Those words snap something inside me. Hearing Fiona begging for my cock is more than I can handle. "You've been mine the moment you were born," I tell her as I line my cock up against her.

Her body tenses, but I coax her to relax with more kisses on her lips. Once she's melted against me again, I begin to push into her.

She gasps into my mouth, but I never stop kissing her as I slowly continue to forge my way inside her tight channel.

Despite how wet she is, she's still virgin tight, and I damn near see stars at the sensation of our bodies becoming one. Her snatch is squeezing my cock so tightly, it's taking every ounce of control I have not to spill prematurely, and I haven't even reached the barrier of her innocence yet.

I still inside her when I reach it, my breath stuttering out. I look down at her flushed face. "You okay, little bird?"

She nods up at me as she says breathily, "It's just so big. I feel so full."

"I've still got more to give you, mate. I'm not even halfway there."

Her eyes widen almost comically. If I wasn't so high strung, I'd chuckle. As it is, all I can do is focus on not spilling my seed inside her before I fully claim her.

When I finally feel halfway back in control, I lean down and begin kissing her again, stroking my tongue in and out of her mouth in a clear imitation of what our bodies are soon to be doing.

She sighs into my mouth, and I take her moment of distraction to finally sheathe myself fully inside her.

I thrust my lips forward, feeling her barrier give way under my intrusion.

She screams into my mouth as I seat myself deep inside her. I groan, her hot, wet channel pulsing around me.

Fuck, she feels incredible. So incredible that I feel my beast snarling and trying to rise to the surface. I struggle to keep him at bay. She's fully human. He'll tear her to pieces if I let him out, and I don't want to hurt her.

I grit my teeth as I fight against him. My vision blurs. I close my eyes and take in deep breaths.

Fiona is clinging to me as her breath comes in little pants. Suddenly, I feel her little hands on either side of my face, and I open my eyes to find those gorgeous sapphires gazing up at me.

"It's okay," she tells me. "You can let him out. I'm not afraid of you or your beast."

My cock jerks within her, and I groan. "You don't know what you're saying, Fiona. My beast is an animal, and he wants to mate you savagely. You're a virgin. Your first time should be slow and gentle." I groan as I grip the side of her neck and gaze down at her wildly. "I won't be able to be soft and tender if I let him out."

She spreads her legs wider, her eyes hooded with lust as she tells me, "I can take it. I *want* it."

Fuck, that's all my beast needs to hear. Her sweet voice calling him forth is too strong. My human side loses the battle, and my beast comes barreling to the front.

I morph, my cock still deep inside her. I watch as her eyes go round when she feels me growing even bigger inside her. What can I say? My beast is even more well-endowed than my human side is.

"Broderick," she moans my name and arches her back up, causing my shaft to shift inside her wet snatch.

I nearly howl with pleasure, the friction lighting up every nerve ending in my body. My beast takes over then, and I begin to hump into her savagely, flexing my hits and pistoning my engorged flesh in and out of her.

"Broderick!" Fiona clings to me as she cries out my name.

I feel the first ripples of her orgasm around me. "Yes!" I snarl, driving into her for all I'm worth, desperate to feel her convulsing all around me as I spill my load inside her.

"Broder—!" she screams my name again, but she loses the last half of it as a high, keening sound overtakes her.

I feel her blossoming open around me, and my cock answers in kind. My balls churn violently before I feel the rush of seed shooting up my stalk. I thrust one last time, howling as I hold myself deep inside her. My staff throbs and pulses until liquid froths from my tip, planting my seed deep inside her fertile womb.

Her head is arched back in bliss, and my mouth falls to her neck, biting her instinctively as waves of pleasure consume us both.

My sac is so full and shoots so much seed inside her that she can't hold it all. I feel my liquid warmth seeping out around our joined bodies, and then my knees finally give out on me as my beast retreats, allowing my human form to come back out.

Mine, mine, mine. I catch myself from falling on her and fall to the side instead. I instantly gather her into my arms, vowing to myself that I'll never let her go again.

"I love you, Fiona, my sweet mate," I tell her as I plant a tender kiss atop her head.

"I love you too, Broderick, my true love," she says as she nuzzles deeper into my chest.

I stroke my hands over her hair, petting her. She once accused me of wanting her as a pet, but she's so much more to me than that, and what she doesn't realize is that my beast will gladly be her pet.

She might as well put a collar on me because she owns me—and my beast—heart and soul.

EPILOGUE

Fiona

My husband reaches over and gives my hand a gentle squeeze, his silvery eyes glowing at me with that special light he reserves only for me. Technically, we didn't have to get married. Fated mates are just that. Mates who are fated to be together. They don't need some big ceremony to seal what they are to one another.

However, Broderick wanted to stay true to my human side too. He knew how much it meant to my papa to see me properly married, so he threw a huge wedding here at the castle. He invited all the townsfolk, and it's amazing how kind people suddenly are to him. It's like seeing my mother's amulet glow for him was all the proof they needed to accept him as one of us.

We were married five years ago. Our wedding was a huge celebration. The townspeople loved it so much that Broderick started opening up his castle to everyone a few times a year. We regularly host balls and dinner parties, and everyone always comes.

Well, almost everyone. Lord Fairchild is not allowed on the premises. My mate's beast won't allow it. He still snarls at even the mention of Fairchild's name, so everyone's careful not to mention the unfortunate lord in his presence.

Broderick invited my father to live at the castle with us, but Papa declined. He didn't want to leave the cottage where he spent the best years of his life with my mother. I also think he didn't want to chance infringing on our privacy. When we're not hosting the entire town at the castle, we're all alone with just us, our child, and the servants.

We're hosting a dinner party at the castle today. I'm sitting at my husband's right hand, as I always do. Tradition may dictate that husband and wife are supposed to sit at opposite ends of the table, but that's where Broderick draws the line. He can't bear to be that far away from me, and the feeling is mutual.

I might not have a beastly side like he does, but the magic of fated mates beats within me too, especially now that Broderick and I are fully mated to one another. I'd been dejected when he sent me away, but it's nothing to the depression that quickly overtakes me when we're parted for very long now that he's claimed my body.

Suffice it to say, Broderick and I are rarely out of sight of one another.

"Mama! Papa!" Lily, our daughter calls out as she comes running up to the table to Broderick and me.

My heart swells within me when Broderick smiles down at her kindly. Whereas most men would have berated the child for interrupting the adult dinner party, he indulges her. Broderick is just as caring and protective of our little girl as he is me—maybe even more so. I shudder to think of how he's going to be when she comes of age and wants to start courting. I'm afraid he's going to scare off every potential mate she has.

I smile to myself. Of course, maybe our

daughter will have a fated mate herself, and then there will be nothing he can do about it.

"What is it, my little flower?" he asks as he gives her his full attention.

"Look! I can transform!" My eyes widen as I watch my daughter morph before my very eyes, white fur sprouting from her body. Her blue eyes seem to become lighter as she turns into a white wolf.

People gasp and ooh and ahh around the table as they take in the sight of our beautiful child. We've been wondering if she would be able to shift like Broderick, though we certainly didn't think she'd be able to do so at so young an age.

I reach out my hand to touch her soft fur, and she nuzzles into my touch.

Broderick's grin is about to split his cheeks as he looks up at me proudly. "I see that! And how beautiful your wolf is!"

It seems Lily only inherited the wolf side of Broderick's beast. She got her sapphire blue eyes from me, but I have no idea where she got her golden blonde hair. It certainly didn't come from me and my raven locks, and Broderick's hair is more of a sandy brown.

"Why don't you shift back and go play with the

other children now?" Broderick suggests to her. Lily's lower lip protrudes out into a pout. This is exciting for her, so she no doubt wants to explore everything in her newly found wolf state.

"But Papa," she begins.

Broderick silences her with a finger to her lips. "My little love, you don't want to make the other children jealous, do you?" he whispers to her conspiratorially. "They can't shift like you can, so it's only polite to stay in your human form while they're around."

She frowns and blinks her innocent little eyes up at him. "But I've seen you shift into your animal form in front of your friends."

I choke back a laugh at the look of shock on Broderick's face.

"That's only when Papa becomes very angry and can't help himself," he admits before placing a kiss on her nose. "Be a good girl and listen to your papa, and I promise you can stay in your wolf form all day tomorrow if you want."

Her eyes light up, and she eagerly nods her head. "Okay, Papa!"

She transforms back into her girlish form and scurries off.

Broderick takes my hand again, his eyes glowing at me warmly.

I nearly melt into a puddle right there at the table with him looking at me like that. Heat blossoms between my legs, and I'm suddenly aching for my husband.

Broderick's nostrils flare, and his eyes darken. He can always sense my desire. We're so in tune to each other's emotions, another effect of our fated mate bond.

He leans over and whispers in my ear, "Keep looking at me like that, Fiona, and I won't care if this dining hall is full of the entire town. I'll spread you out on this table and breed you right here, my mate."

My breath catches in my throat, and my face flames. I'm sure that everyone will be able to discern the nature of the filth my husband is whispering in my ear by the color of my cheeks alone.

He chuckles before he pushes my hair back from my shoulder to reveal his bite mark for all to see. Broderick's beast becomes more possessive when he knows we're going to have company. He likes to sink his teeth into my neck and leave a visible mark on me for all to see, and the beast must be struggling to come out to play now for

Broderick to be baring my mark for the entire table to see.

Although my face flushes, I hold my head high, wearing my husband's mark with pride.

I feel the warm glow from the amulet against my skin. I always wear it when we have company, knowing how Broderick likes for the entire town to see my love for him literally glowing around my neck.

Me stumbling across Broderick that day was fate—even if neither one of us recognized it at the time.

I see Broderick's silvery gray eyes land on my amulet, and my heart glows with love as the glow in my mate's eyes rivals that of the stone.

I'm so glad I was fated to the beast.

Hey there, you gorgeous reading machine!

First of all, THANK YOU for spending your precious time with my characters and letting me take up space in your brain for a while. You could've been doing literally anything else—like scrolling social media or alphabetizing your spice rack—but instead, you chose this. And I love you for it.

Now, let me let you in on a little secret: I'm basically the romance writing equivalent of a shapeshifter. One author, multiple personalities. Here are the pen names I write under:

- Emma Bray — steamy contemporary romance that's all heart eyes and heat
- Kenzie Skye — spicy romantasy and paranormal goodness—magic, monsters, and all the feels
- DAHLIA — downright filthy, dirty, naughty erotic romance (It's okay if you like it. I won't tell. 🫢)
- E.B. Fox — dark, broody, edge-of-your-seat romance for when you want to walk on the wild side

Craving more? Head to www.spicy-romance.com and sign up for my newsletter. As a thank-you, you'll get a free book you can't find anywhere else. (Check out this preview to get a sample of it.)

And I promise, cross my heart and swear on my sexiest plot twist: I will NEVER spam you. Only juicy updates, exclusive goodies, and sneak peeks that'll leave you begging for more.

Stay spicy, stay amazing, and keep chasing those happily ever afters (or wickedly dark ones—no judgment).

Big hugs and even bigger love,

The romance writing shapeshifter

P.S. Did I mention you're awesome? Because you are. 

P.S.S. Here are some super handy-dandy lists where you can find all of my books:

- books2read.com/rl/emmabray
- books2read.com/rl/kenzieskye
- books2read.com/rl/dahlia
- books2read.com/rl/ebfox

~

Keep reading for an excerpt from the next book in the Steamy Shifters series: Charming the Dragon.

CHARMING THE DRAGON

"I'm sorry about this, girl. We're just following orders," the hulking guard to my left of me says.

"Yeah, you heard what the oracle said," the other one chimes in from my right. Yeah, I heard what the oracle said, and I'd like to rip the bitch's eyes and hair out.

I'm sandwiched in between the huge men, each of them holding onto one of my arms like they're afraid I'm going to make a run for it. They don't need to worry about that, though. I understand my responsibility to the village, and I wouldn't try to shirk my duty that way.

I took my fate with dignity. I didn't break down and cry and make a commotion when the oracle announced that I was the virgin who was going to be sacrificed to the dragon up on Fire Mountain.

Yeah, not only is it bad enough that I'm the unlucky girl who gets to be sacrificed to the fearsome, fire-breathing dragon, but that oracle just outed me in front of the whole town for being a virgin. That's not really something I wanted the entire village to know, but I guess it won't matter whenever I become dragon food.

I don't exactly know what's going to happen up on the mountain, but that's what I assume it's going to be anyway.

Legend has it that no virgin has ever come down from the mountain after being taken up. Of course, that can't really be confirmed since one is only sent up every one hundred years.

Lucky me that I would be alive on the centennial that a new one is chosen. And with my shitty luck, I would be the one chosen.

I'd be lying if I said I wasn't a little scared, but what concerns me the most isn't my own fate. If I'm going to be eaten by a dragon, no amount of moping and whining about it is going to change it. No, what worries me the most is who's going to take care of my little sister now that I'm gone?

I just turned eighteen, but my sister is only

fourteen. Both of our parents died of the fever a couple of years ago, so it's just the two of us. I can't stand the thought of some old pervert getting his hands on her, but I know that with me out of the picture, marrying early is going to be about the only thing that will save her.

The irony of the situation isn't lost on me. I'm wearing a gorgeous dress of light, peachy pink that flows all the way down to my ankles. It's strapless and held up by my petite bosom. My honey-colored hair was brushed until it shone and left to cascade freely down my shoulders.

It's like the townsfolk wanted to make sure I looked really pretty for my funeral. Maybe dragons only want to eat pretty things. I don't know.

I look up at the fiery mountain top. I can't help but think that Fire Mountain is aptly named. The closer we get to the top of the mountain, the hotter it gets, which is just the opposite of how it usually is. It's usually colder on mountaintops, but not up here on Fire Mountain. I guess it's the dragon. He must generate so much heat that it keeps it warmer up here.

I don't know which death would be more preferable—combusting to death from the heat or being eaten alive by an enormous dragon.

I guess I'll find out soon enough because we're almost at the top.

When we reach the mouth of the cave, I can feel the two men trembling from where they each grip my arms. I have to suppress a wry grin. Shouldn't *I* be the one trembling? What are they so scared for? They get to go back home to their families. I'm the one being left up here with the dragon.

They deposit me at the mouth of the cave and then shuffle their feet like the cowards they are, casting me pitying, sorrowful glances. "We're real sorry about this, girl," they tell me. To their credit, they truly do seem to mean their words.

"Macy," I tell them.

They blink and look at me questioningly.

"My name is Macy," I elaborate. "I figure it would be kind of sad for the last people I see to not even know my name, so there it is."

The men stare at me in horror, and neither offers to tell me his name. I guess they figure what's the point.

Oh well.

I take pity on them and don't make it too hard on them. I know they're just following orders and that it would have been their necks too if they hadn't agreed to drag me up here. Not that they'd had to drag me. I came readily enough, but still.

I wave my hand at them cheerily, "Oh, perk up boys. Don't worry about me. I'll be fine."

They cast dubious glances at one another. "Are you sure you're alright, girl?" one of them asks me, obviously thinking that I've already gone mad. I notice he doesn't speak my name, but that's okay.

My smile only widens. "Of course. Why wouldn't I be? I'm happy to be sacrificed for my village!" I make my voice bright and cheery.

The two befuddled men share another glance with one another. They obviously don't feel good about leaving me in this state, which is ironic because would they feel better if I were in hysterics, sobbing and kicking and screaming? Something tells me they would, that my positive attitude is worse for them than the alternative. I guess because it's not predictable, and men don't like a woman who's not predictable or who doesn't fit their mold.

On second thought, it's probably for the best that I'm the one being sacrificed to a dragon because I never would have fit the mold of the perfect housewife that would have been expected of me had I stayed in the village. I suppose, all things considered, this does work out the way it should. I still want to strangle that oracle, though.

I smile before I clap my hands together in excitement. "Now where's this fire-breathing dragon I'm supposed to meet?"

"Right here," a booming voice thunders.

Keep reading Charming the Dragon here: https://books2read.com/charmingthedragon

SEX AND CANDY - EXCLUSIVE FREEBIE

She's too sweet to resist. And she's mine. All mine.

Ace

Three things are for sure:

One: She's the most stunning little thing I've ever laid eyes on.

Two: She doesn't belong on that stage, shaking it for men who don't deserve to breathe her air.

Three: She's already mine—even if she doesn't know it yet.

And I don't care what I have to do to prove it.

Candy

Only two things in life are for sure:

One: Nothing in life comes without a price.

Two: Men only ever want one thing.

But Ace? He's not like the others. He's dangerous, possessive, and makes promises I've never heard before. I should run... but every instinct in me tells me to stay.

Sex and Candy is a *steamy-as-sin* romance featuring an obsessive billionaire alpha who will do anything—*anything*—to claim his woman. He's intense, over-the-top, and completely irresistible. Protective? Yes. Possessive? Hell yes. HEA? Always.

Keep reading for a preview of Sex and Candy:

. . .

I take a sip of the subpar whiskey in front of me and grimace at the taste as I glance down at my Rolex. Fucker's late.

I drum my fingers on the table in irritation, keenly reminded of why I never let anyone pick meeting locations. You never know what kind of seedy joint they're going to want to meet up in or if they'll even show up at all.

I knew better than to let MacHay dictate the terms of this meeting, but I went against my better instincts and did it anyway. Simply because the man has proven so difficult to get in touch with. I'm regretting ever shaking his hand in the first place, and if I wasn't beholden to hold up my end of the bargain, I'd say fuck it and bail on this here and now.

Oh, well. You live and learn, right?

I'm tempted to do it anyway and am actually moving to slip out of my booth when the stage lights up and a hush falls over the audience.

I don't know what causes me to pause and sit back down. It's probably just going to be another subpar dancer like all the other ones that have been staggering around on the stage all night.

Maybe it's the pregnant pause of anticipation that seems to fall over the entire room.

I don't know.

But when the tiniest little angel I've ever seen steps on stage, time itself seems to stop.

Her skin glows ivory under the stage light. She has on a lacy white number, some sort of bustier, lacy panties, and white stockings. The look is topped off with fire engine red heels that match the paint on her lips. Long lashes frame light brown eyes that look too big and luminous for her little heart-shaped face. Long blonde hair like spun gold falls in glorious waves all the way down to an impossibly tiny waist that I know I could cup in my two hands. My breath catches in my throat. My god, she looks like a porcelain doll come to life.

But what most arrests me is the look in her eyes. For a split second when she first steps out on stage, her wide eyes are soulfully sad, so much so that they seem to take my breath away.

They seem to mirror all the tragedy in the world in their depths.

But then it's gone in the blink of an eye as she smiles, a dazzling, heart-wrenching smile that makes me instantly jealous. I'm irrationally upset that's she's gracing this roomful of men with that smile—that smile that I suddenly know deep down in my soul is meant to be only mine.

Mine.

Sultry music begins to play, and she begins to dance, gently swaying her hips as she flirts with the strip pole.

I'm gripping the edge of the table so tightly I'm surprised the wood doesn't break underneath my palms. I swear to God if one piece of clothing comes off her body I won't be able to stop myself from rushing up on that stage and covering her from prying eyes.

I'm aware that my reaction is insane. I don't know anything about this girl, but I can't stop the surge of possessive protectiveness that rages inside me at the thought of all these men seeing her so scantily clad like this.

What the fuck is she doing? Doesn't she know she's an angel? Doesn't she know she doesn't belong in here with all these devils?

I grit my teeth when she suddenly flings herself on the pole and begins to do a series of complicated flips and turns. The men roar and whistle and cheer, and I'd bet my last million half the fuckers in this place have a boner right now imagining her little body writhing on their laps like she is on that pole.

The thought fills me with murderous rage.

I'm so distracted by it that I don't even notice when MacHay finally takes his seat across from me until he chuckles and comments, "It's your first time witnessing the wonder that is Candy, huh?"

"What?" I bark at him, never tearing my eyes away from the beauty up on the stage. I feel like I won't be able to rest until her set is over and she's safely back behind that stage curtain where she belongs out of sight of lascivious male eyes.

He juts his chin out at the stage. "Candy. She's the feature dancer here." I spare a sideways glance at him out of the corner of my eye. He takes a sip of his drink and motions toward the stage with it, "And you can see why. Not only is she the prettiest one out of the bunch, but she's also the youngest and the one with the most skill. Consequently, she's the one Dan hoards to himself like the finest treasure. You can pay for a little extra with the other dancers, if you know what I mean, but Dan won't let anyone near Candy for no amount of money."

I frown, though I can't help feeling some sort of relief at the thought that Candy isn't being prostituted out. I can barely stomach the thought of all these men's eyes on her, much less their hands.

"So," MacHay rubs his hands together eagerly as Candy's show ends and she leaves the stage. I notice how she doesn't scramble to pick up any of the money thrown on the stage for her like all the dancers before her did. She walks coolly off the stage without even a backward glance at all the men she now holds in her thrall. "You really to get down to business?" MacHay interrupts my thoughts.

I scowl at him. The fucker keeps me waiting all the time, and then he shows up and expects me to cater to him. He can fucking wait now.

I level him with a cool stare before I stand from the booth and pull out my phone. "I have something to attend to first. If you want to see any part of this partnership go forward, you'll be sitting right here waiting for me when I get back."

He frowns and looks like he wants to say something, but one look at my tight jawline and he obviously thinks better of it, giving a curt nod of understanding instead. Yeah, he knows he fucked up.

I step out of earshot and call my head of security.

"Yeah, James? Get me everything you can on a dancer at the club on Sixth. Pronto. I want everything within the next thirty minutes. Goes by the name of Candy..."

Get your exclusive copy of Sex and Candy by signing up for my newsletter here: www.spicy-romance.com.

www.ingramcontent.com/pod-product-compliance
Lightning Source LLC
Chambersburg PA
CBHW031314160726
47993CB00001B/420